The Droll Teller

By

S. E. England

ISBN: 979-8-3740-5791-1

1st Edition
www.sarahenglandauthor.co.uk

TALES OF THE OCCULT BY SARAH E. ENGLAND

ABOUT THE AUTHOR

Sarah England is a UK author with a background in nursing and psychiatry, a theme which creeps into many of her stories. At the fore of Sarah's body of work is the bestselling occult horror trilogy, *Father of Lies, Tanners Dell,* and *Magda*, followed by a spin-off from the series, *The Owlmen*. Other novels include *The Soprano, Hidden Company, Monkspike, Baba Lenka, Masquerade, Caduceus,* and *Groom Lake. The Witching Hour* is a collection of short stories; and *The Droll Teller,* a ghostly novella, is her latest book.

If you would like to be informed about future releases, there is a newsletter sign-up on Sarah's website. Please feel free to get in touch – it would be great to hear from you!

www.sarahenglandauthor.co.uk

PROLOGUE

Gorse Bank House, Devon.
Christmas, 1962

I was ten, it was the middle of the night, and I woke suddenly with a bang to the heart. Not from a deep, wholesome sleep either, but from a state of drifting in outer darkness. A vague dread had been infiltrating my consciousness for some time, an awareness of another presence… and the sound of water…. Of someone or something splashing water…

My eyes snapped open.

The bedroom, in which I slept alone, was gloomy, curtains drawn against the Devon moorland and the cold, bleak hush that preceded a wintry dawn. I lay utterly motionless, feet pressing into a hot water bottle that had long since cooled, eyes adjusting to the gloom. And then, in a spider's thread of silvery light, I caught a movement.

A thud of sickly fear followed the initial shock, as my gaze then settled on the faint silhouette of a figure hunched over the wash basin in the corner. Wearing an antiquated white corset in the style once worn under a full-skirted long dress, a woman was scrubbing at her hands and forearms with immense concentration and intensity of purpose. An occasional sob broke out as, with her head bent over the basin, she furiously excoriated her skin with a nail brush. Pausing to examine the results, seemingly dissatisfied, she then plunged her hands back into the water, before resuming.

I lay stone-rigid, hardly daring to breathe, could not afford to make the slightest sound in case she noticed, yet nor could I take my eyes from the apparition, or shut out the scene and pretend it wasn't happening. It was a ghost, most definitely, it had to be. Ivy and Beatrice at the farm had said the house was haunted but I'd only half believed it. Torn. And my mother had been annoyed at the suggestion. Dad had laughed out loud. No ghosts, no. Ridiculous.

What was a ghost exactly, I'd wanted to know.

"A dead person," Beatrice had said. "Dead and evil, come to get you."

But Beatrice, a couple of years older than me, had also laughed. It was a joke. Wasn't it? Just a joke… Except now it wasn't. I blinked and blinked again, considering this might be part of a dream and not real. But an overpowering scent had also permeated the room, that of sickly-sweet violets; and the light seemed strangely intense, brighter than before, charged with static as if a television set had been left on.

In the end though, I could hold my breath no longer, and the small sigh that seeped from my lungs seemed to my ears a cacophony in the silence of the night.

Instantly, the ghostly stranger's head jerked up. The woman was staring directly into the small oval mirror positioned over the washstand. And my child's heart speeded up, thumping hard in my chest.

Don't see me… don't look at me… please don't…

But she did.

The haggard, blue-white face seemed to wear the stamp of something not quite human, as she stood poised with the nail brush, frozen mid-movement. And then slowly, oh-so-slowly, the feverish, unnaturally glittering eyes alighted on me, as I lay in the single bed by the wall. An expression of speechless horror followed, as the wild fascinated stare met mine.

I'd been paralysed, unable to think, unable to move. When without warning, the apparition swung round to face me in one sharp movement.

And only then did the terror rip out of my lungs – a bloodcurdling scream that rent the icy blue air, echoing through the cavernous rooms of the house, and had my father thundering up the stairs two at a time.

"Enys! Enys! What the hell…?"

***

PART ONE
Enys Quiller, December 1962

'By the fruits of the tree ye shall know them...'
Bible Verse

CHAPTER ONE

Enys Quiller's Story

1962 was a memorable year for many reasons – the Cuban missile crisis, Marilyn Monroe singing, 'Happy Birthday, Mr President' to John F. Kennedy at Madison Square Garden in New York, and The Beatles' hit single, *Love Me Do*. A thousand memories rush back to me every time I hear it. But for our family, the memory of that particular year was permanently ingrained for a wholly different reason.

I was ten the Christmas our lives changed forever. Elvis was at Number One with *Return to Sender*, which Dad said would have been a good one to play at Great Aunt Mary's funeral, and Mum had just found out we'd inherited Gorse Bank House in Devon. I remember her answering the phone in the hall, standing at the little table by the front door, the Christmas tree lights a blur of pink, blue and green through the frosted glass partition. I'd been cutting out paperchains, and Dad was singing, 'I can't stop loving you,' while he did the washing-up, elbow deep in suds when she came slowly back in, ashen-faced, and gave us the news.

"Mary's gone. Died the night before last. That was Ivy Trove."

"Who's Mary?"

"Shush, Enys," my mother said, eyes fixed on Dad.

He'd dried his hands on a tea towel and was walking towards her, I thought to hug her. He was famous for his bear hugs. I'd glanced up, can still see the back of his neck, clean-shaven, the white collar of his work shirt. But she stepped back, eyes gleaming with what I mistook at the time for grief. The kaleidoscope of my world was at that moment about to change, all known components given a damn good shake-up, and when they settled again it would be in a completely different pattern. But I was not to know that yet. All I knew was something was wrong, and a physical sensation like a small clenched fist formed in the pit of my stomach as I watched her recoil from my dad. I'd never heard of this Mary. Mum had never spoken of her, and rarely had she mentioned Ivy Trove, at least not without tightening her lips to spit out the name. Yet suddenly Mary was monumentally important, my mother so shocked she had to sit down.

"What's the matter?" said Dad.

"Mary left everything to me, Jimmy – the house, the estate, the money – the whole lot."

For what seemed like forever, no words passed between them. My glance shot from one to the other. What did it mean? Was this good or bad? Her eyes were wide as she stared at him, just staring and staring. The moment was unbearable, like waiting for an elastic band to be stretched to breaking point. Eventually there'd be a painful twang.

At last Dad cleared his throat. "And that's official, is it? How would Ivy know?"

That did it, his words broke the trance. My mother threw her hands into the air and yelled, "How the bloody hell should I know?"

"Hey, steady on. I only–"

But when she took off on a verbal tirade, she was never able to stop, and experience dictated the only course of action was to let her run and run until she was all emptied out. Dad leaned back against the sink, tea towel still in hand, for the long haul.

"That's just like you to start questioning me as if I made it up, that I must have got it all wrong, that I'm missing a cerebral lobe. That's you all over. But I know what I just heard, and I'll tell you something else for free – I know Ivy Trove and you can bet your bottom dollar it would have cost her to ring up and tell me that. She'd have had to, of course. Who else? That sop wit of a husband of hers – Georgy Porgy? Or a high and mighty Hamlyn? Ha! Can you imagine?" She put both hands to her face, and I saw then the secret glee. "Little Josie Nobody got the lot. Oh, my good God! I bet she really, really badly didn't want to tell me that."

On and on she went. I can't remember the exact words any more, but I got the gist. How jealous and spiteful Ivy Trove had been. How Mum had been forced to leave the farm she grew up in at just eighteen to escape, how she'd had no help from anyone in the family and been left to fend for herself. Anything could have happened to her as a nurse in London, while Ivy, poison Ivy, fat Ivy, had stayed home, baked cakes and milked cows. And did any single one of them give a tinker's cuss, while she was mopping up blood and sick? No. She'd not had enough to eat, did they know that? Sometimes couldn't afford the tube fare home when she was dead on her feet. No, no, they couldn't have cared less.

I realise now, decades later, that she'd genuinely been abandoned, and had absolutely felt the very real fear of being a young woman alone, without money or family support; but rarely did more than a couple of weeks go by without the same story being told, and Dad and I knew it inside out and back to front. We hung our heads that night as we always did, not knowing what to say, when just as abruptly the mood swung back again. To shock, elation, excitement, disbelief.

"So, I got Gorse Bank House, then. Bloody hell! I mean, bloody hell, Jimmy!"

She'd finally run out of steam, had stopped twisting the hem of her blue gingham pinny, and was staring blankly into the middle distance.

The only sounds were the spatter of sleety snow against the kitchen window, and the whir of the rapidly cooling oven.

Then suddenly she turned to Dad. "Anyway," she said. "We'll need to start packing. Now, tonight."

Pack?

She started to talk again, in rapid fire, but I have no idea what was said. I'd stopped sticking rings of coloured paper together, remember thinking instead, 'But what about the Christmas tree, and the cake we've got to ice tomorrow, and all the presents Father Christmas is supposed to leave at this particular house down this particular chimney?' She'd said to pack. So close to Christmas. And then there was the carol service, and I was an angel in the nativity play…

"Hang on a minute, Josie. We're not going anywhere

tonight. The shop–"

She stood up. "No! Don't you see, Jim? Don't you get it? Hasn't it dawned on you, yet? My great aunt Mary was as rich as bloody Croesus. You won't ever have to worry about money again. You won't have to work. It's a huge house. A ruddy great big house with dozens of acres, a river, barns and stables."

The shock was palpable.

I saw then, in my mind's eye, Dad's chemist shop with its rows and rows of miniature wooden drawers filled with hand-written notes, all in alphabetical order; the locked cabinets, pestles, scales, glass vials and syringes in cases fastened with clasps. In a heartbeat I was back on the row of seats by the window waiting for him, breathing in the powdery scents of lavender and rose, intermingled with Vicks vapour rub. Quiller's Pharmacy stood on the corner of the high street, just along from where we lived in Camden Town. On the long wooden counter there were oversized jars full of lollipops for anxious or bored children, there were flannels and sponges, toothbrushes and soaps, lozenges for sore throats, and gondolas stacked with bottles of shampoo, rollers and hairnets. Sparkles of dust danced in the air on drowsy afternoons, golden light falling in slats through the new blinds. And at the clang of a bell when the door opened from the street, Dad would emerge through a curtain of multi-coloured ribbons from the back room, the lab he called it, with a small box of pills or a syrupy elixir in a brown glass jar.

'Here you go, kill or cure, the secret's in the dose,' he'd say, patiently repeating precise instructions – my tall, lanky, sandy-haired dad, peering over the top of his spectacles. It was who he was. Everything. And the customers loved him, knew him, respected him and asked for his advice.

My mother's voice broke the reverie.

"We'll have to go as soon as possible, the funeral's on Friday. Why don't you ring what's-his-name to cover? You close over Christmas anyway and it's only for a few days. He'll do it – Clive, that's it. Ring him now!"

I was going to play the lead angel on Thursday, the day before school broke up for the holiday, and she was talking about us leaving straight away, to go somewhere miles and miles away that I'd barely heard of, and at Christmas, too. I think I was crying, vaguely recall throwing a mass of paper to the floor, telling her I had to play the Angel Gabriel. We'd made a costume. She couldn't have forgotten. No one else knew the words. I had to go. I wanted to wear the white dress and the golden wings… wanted to so badly… to walk onto the stage and say the line I'd rehearsed a hundred times. And there was a disco afterwards with sandwiches and cakes. Everyone in class had been asked to make something…

Neither of them even glanced at me, and I felt then, things slipping away.

Dad was glowering, his face pale and stony; but my mother… oh, my mother was shaking – cheeks aflame, eyes bright as a blackbird's. She was focused entirely on him, and I knew she'd scream and cry if he objected. A lot of the time we both instinctively tried to stop her from crying, or shouting. My dad's soothing voice, his arm around her, was one of the abiding images I had of those years in Camden. Before we went to Devon.

But in the end, none of us, including her, could have known, even as suitcases and bags were thrown into the boot of the old Vauxhall Victor on Thursday night, how that Christmas would shatter our lives so irrevocably. Not just in a practical, physical way, but fundamentally – deeply, psychologically – perhaps for my dad most of all. But none of us had the least idea of what was coming.

***

CHAPTER TWO

I'm telling the story now as I recall it, looking back sixty years, filling in some of the gaps from what I've been told by others along the way. We all remember conversations and the order in which things happened slightly differently, but the upshot's the same in the end, and so here it is, right down to how it upset us all so badly we were never the same again. And not one of us escaped that, not one...

Anyway, the next clear memory I have was of sitting on the back seat of my dad's old Vauxhall Victor as we sped towards Devon. I know I got to play the Angel Gabriel because I still had the foil halo on, along with a maroon gaberdine I had to wear for school. I'm guessing we ate on the way.

"Count the Christmas trees, Enys. There's one, look!"

I kept my head absolutely motionless, focusing on my wraith-like reflection in the passenger window as amber lights whooshed by, until before long the sprawling suburbs were in the rear-view mirror, and all around was disorientating darkness.

"You're not going to be sick, are you, Enys?"

I was never not travel sick in that car. It always smelled of petrol.

"She's gone quiet. She looks green, Jimmy."

"Do you want me to stop, sweetheart?"

"Don't you dare be sick on the upholstery. Say if you need to stop." She looked at her watch. "We've got hours to go yet."

"Enys, do you need to be sick? Josie, tissues are in the glove compartment."

I said nothing, never did, had to keep my mouth firmly closed, repeatedly swallowing. It was always the same on the back seat. "Uh-uh."

"You'd better be sure."

Devon seemed an extremely long way off. Hours passed, fog rolled off the moors, and at times it felt as if ours was the only car on the road, that we were suspended in time. Occasionally, the sight of a homely-looking lamp lifted my hopes that we were almost there, only to vanish again. It was cold, I wished I was at home in bed, and probably, eventually, I drowsed.

When next I woke it was to the rumble of the road, a sea of grey at every window, and the red glow of tail lights reflected in the fog behind.

"Are we in Devon yet?"

"Yes," Dad said. "Past Exeter now, but it's a big county, way to go yet."

Fog had blanketed the surrounding moorland, rolling over us in banks.

"Do you know the way once we come off at Okehampton?"

"Head for Gulston," my mother said. "I'll say when we get to the turn-off."

It could be that's when my fascination with ancient stories began, because my mother was a good storyteller and tales of highwaymen broke the monotony. From time to time we passed a pub, long, low thatches with white cob walls flush to the kerb – travellers' havens with strings of coloured lights swinging outside. Like lit galleons on an inky ocean that rose and swelled as hills and dales, they fired my imagination. The Vauxhall thumped into each lump in the road, me clutching onto the headrest in front to stop myself from sliding across the back seat, listening intently to my mother as she held me, rapt, in another time, another place.

She'd never talked much about where she came from, and we'd never been to visit the few relatives she had, either. Up to that point they hadn't played any part in our lives whatsoever and were not part of my existence. As such I'd never given any of them a thought. I was from London, my dad's family were all in London, and that's where I lived and went to school, where all my friends were. That was it. The only time the relatives in Devon were mentioned was at Christmas and birthdays when a card was sent to me with a pound note in it from 'Auntie Ivy, Uncle George and Cousin Beatrice' – a mysterious faceless family from the 'back of beyond' as my mother called Hunters Combe. And no wonder, the way she described it.

My mother and Ivy had actually grown up together on a 'God-forsaken farm knee-deep in cow muck'. She painted a picture of the most bleak and miserable place imaginable, where mice scooted across the floor at night, and it was so cold and damp she'd had chilblains. And as a teen, to get to any of the dance halls she'd had to take a slow, chugging bus that smelled of diesel fumes over the hills to Gulston. It took so long that no sooner had she arrived and queued to hand her coat in, it was time to set off back. It sounded terrible. Not like London, where there were loads of nice places to eat and drink and shop, all warm, well-lit and close together, so modern and exciting.

"And as for that Ivy, I hated having to share a room with a little kid when I was a teen. Can you imagine?"

I shook my head. It was obvious, though, how much she didn't like her only sister. But at least I'd heard of her, unlike my mother's parents, a set of grandparents never mentioned. The only grandparents I knew about were on my dad's side. As for the Great Aunt Mary character – well, she'd loomed out of the blue, and now she was dead.

Dad remembers me pestering my mother, bombarding her with questions, and although he was glad in a way, he could see she was getting agitated and he needed to concentrate on an increasingly difficult and tiring drive.

"So how old was Great Aunt Mary?" I said to the back of my mother's neat, brunette, Jackie Kennedy hairstyle.

"Ninety."

"Ninety? That's means she was an antique, doesn't it? Was she all alone in the massive big house? Why didn't anyone else live with her there? Wasn't she lonely? What was she like? And–"

"I think I've missed a turning somewhere." High on Dartmoor by then, we'd slowed to a crawl, squinting into a wall of fog. "I'll have to pull over."

He swerved sharply into a layby that was suddenly upon us, switched off the engine and flicked on the overhead light to look at the map. And that was another moment I'll not forget – the silence, after hours and hours of the drum of the road.

A keen wind whined over the moors, pummelling the car.

"Are we lost, Mum?"

It was a first for me, to feel a pinch of fear, insecurity.

"No," she said, vaguely. "I just don't know where we are."

Dad laughed, and then she clicked into gear. "Oh, I know, we've overshot Hobbs Lane. I didn't see The Tailor's Rest. It must be closed. That's right then, carry on up here past Hounds Tor. It'll get steep and you'll see the old chimney where the mine used to be, but after that the road winds down to the coast, and the house is about halfway along. We don't go through the village this way, that's all. Anyway, it's not far now. I know where we are, we're not lost."

The coast? That's the word that leapt out at me. I'd never seen the sea, not even for a day trip. The sea… the house was near the sea…

"You can understand why I wanted to get away now, can't you, Enys?" Mum said over her shoulder. "Look how bleak it is! How lonely. We're nearly at the Cornish border, almost on it, we are."

"Not that lonely – you were in a village, weren't you? On a farm, and there was your sister, Ivy–" Dad said, re-starting the engine.

And that was another first: my mother's accent changed in a heartbeat, as if she was a different person altogether. The words snapped out with vehemence, "She'm not my sister."

"What do you–?"

He didn't get the chance to question her further, however, because Hounds Tor summit was hazardous, in thick, wet fog with a sheer drop of granite scree on one side. All conversation died. And not until we'd begun the descent, and the zig-zag lane began to straggle down to the valley, did any of us breathe easy again.

And then all at once, there it was.

About halfway down, just as my mother had described, stood Great Aunt Mary's house. Two immense gateposts appeared to rise out of the fog before us.

Dad sounded weary. "This it?"

Gorse Bank House was set fairly close to the road, tall and narrow, built of stone now weathered black. It was alone on the hill, and had an unusual triangular pediment in the centre with a circular window inset with a lead cross. It was unlit, no streetlights, the night coalface black. And there was nothing welcoming about it at all.

"She could at least have switched a lamp on," my mother grumbled as we parked in the drive.

After she got out, Dad and I sat for a while. Adjusting. While my mother went to find the key Ivy was supposed to have left inside the porch.

"It'll all look different tomorrow," he said eventually.

And it did. Oh, it definitely did.

***

CHAPTER THREE

We all slept in the same room that first night, bundled into sleeping bags, exhausted. There wasn't any central heating, that was for sure, but then we hadn't any in London either, and I didn't know anyone who had. But Gorse Bank House was far colder than anything I'd previously experienced, possessing the all-pervasive damp chill of a church crypt.

It was the next day, however, when we met up with Ivy Trove, and notably for me, her daughter Beatrice, that was most memorable. That really shook things up. Let's just say I was innocent when we set off down the lane, and not quite so much on the way back. Before I met Beatrice there were questions I never knew existed, let alone thought to ask.

The morning was bright and clear, fields and moors washed clean, cobweb-laced hedgerows sparkling with globes of dew. Stepping outside was a pleasant surprise, being several degrees warmer than within. The house had been built to withstand blasting winds off the Atlantic to the north, and Dartmoor to the east. But below it, in vivid contrast to the harsh landscape of the moors, lay a lush and sylvan valley. Just a short walk down the lane and the whipping wind dropped to a soft sigh, high hedges providing a shield, the air so balmy in the sun it could almost have been spring.

"There'll be daffs out by January," my mother said, as we tramped towards the village for the funeral. "Very warm in these parts. Next village is in Cornwall. We'll have to take you to see the sea, Enys."

She seemed nervous, her speech clipped and unnatural, as holding onto her hat with one hand she clutched a little Jackie Kennedy handbag with the other. Straight out of a magazine, was how Dad said she looked. Frosted, pale pink lipstick completed the picture, and pin-neat kitten heels. Goodness knows what I had on, nothing black, maybe my maroon school gabardine? Oh, and white knee socks. She was talking about the Atlantic coastline, telling stories about wreckers and smugglers, about pepper holes or spouts – channels that ran inside the cliff down to the bay – and how ships would get caught in the crosswinds and smash on the rocks, cargo floating in the waves. By the time we rounded the corner into Hunters Combe my mind was full of villagers on stormy beaches at midnight, dragging kegs onto the shore, hurriedly stashing the booty in caves.

"They brought the heavy loads up on donkeys' backs," she said, "all the way up to the mine shafts. Look there at the name – Donkey Lane!"

She was, as I said, a good storyteller, embellishing each tale in the re-telling. I was entranced anyway, my already suggestible imagination on overload. What magical wonderland had we come to? I felt my spirits pick up – excited, I suppose.

We were on foot that morning because of the narrowness of the lanes, which were barely wide enough for a pony and trap, and there were no passing places. So we walked into the village and I took it all in, surprised at how big it was, how clean, how pretty, not at all the image of desolation my mother had painted. It wasn't like she'd said at all. I was coming to realise round about then that she worked hard at getting people to see things the way she wanted them to, and not necessarily the way they actually were. White-walled thatched cottages bordered both sides of the main road, with more visible up various hilly tracks. And at the far end was a church, with just enough room for a hearse to park outside the wooden gates. I don't recall seeing any cars, and if there were, then where were they kept? Nowadays there's an art gallery where the old post office used to be, and the mill by the stream is a trendy gastro pub complete with a car park instead of the old dancing green; but back then, Hunters Combe was bustling with people and all the cottages had front doors flung wide, women in aprons and stout boots chatting on the doorsteps as we walked past.

"'Ere, if it isn't Josie Trewhella!"

It struck me that my mother was some kind of celebrity, everyone seemed to know her, and my face flamed. I think my dad's did, too.

At every house it was the same. They were sorry to hear about Great Aunt Mary, and wasn't it sad? Mind you, ee'd been a ripe old age, hadn't ee?

My mother pushed me forwards. This was James Quiller, her husband, and Enys, her daughter. "Say 'hello', Enys."

"Ah, shy, is she? Look how rosy she be!"

"Well, ee looks very smart Josie. Put us all to shame. That London-made, is it?"

"The dress and coat? No, I made them myself. Well, cut from a pattern… Anyway, we must press on, we haven't much time and I don't want us to be late."

"Over to Ivy's, are you?"

"That's right."

She was holding my hand, squeezing it tightly, already pulling away.

"They seem nice," my dad said, once we were out of earshot.

She glanced at her watch, speeding up. "That's the problem with these small villages," my mother snapped. "Always poking into everyone else's business. Everyone knows everything about everyone else. Ivy this and Ivy that. Drives you mad, it does."

The pace picked up to the point I was nearly running along to the smart click-click-click of kitten heels. My mother was granite-faced and there certainly weren't any more stories about smugglers and pirates. In fact, there were no words at all and my dad vouched for that many, many years later.

We continued past the church, out of the village, and were into pasture land before my mother finally stopped. There on the left, by the gates to a long straight drive, was a tumble of milk churns and a hand-painted sign for Trewhella Farm. She took several deep breaths, seeming to draw herself up. I thought she was scared of having to see poison Ivy, fat Ivy, the spoilt girl who'd made her young life so unbearable, causing her to leave home and take a bus all the way to London. How terrible for her to have to come back and be subjected to this woman. The sooner we could sell the big house and go home, the better. She just had to get this over with. Poor Mum! I felt all those emotions and more, made a move to put my hand in hers...

But her next words jarred and stuck, shattering once

more the contents of the kaleidoscope that had not yet settled after the initial shake-up. And she spoke them in that strangely thick, clotted cream accent she'd used the previous night, the one I'd never heard her use before.

Ignoring me altogether, she faced my dad. "Right, James Quiller. And I mean this, so listen good and hard. Don't you dare gawp at her, all right? Don't you dare go all puppy-eyed looking at Ivy Trove or I swear to God, I will never forgive you."

Dad's mouth dropped open.

"You think I'm joking? She'm a blousy piece of work. Got knocked up out of wedlock with thick-as-pudding George 'ere, who was forced to marry her. So, you give 'er the glad eye and you can 'ave a separate bedroom for the rest of your life, and don't think–"

She'd started and couldn't stop.

Dad took hold of her elbow and walked her further down the lane, hissing at her to give over, would she? It was several minutes before she'd calmed down enough to walk back again, and when she did she was pinched and pasty-looking. She really and truly did not want to go back to the farm. If you've ever seen a cat that didn't want to be held, body stiff as rigor mortis, eyes staring and wild – that was her.

It never occurred to me for one minute, however, that this poisonous sister would turn out to be one of the most strikingly beautiful human beings I would ever see, either on screen or off. But she was. So was her daughter, Beatrice, a girl barely on the cusp of womanhood, although you could see plainly enough how she'd ease into the role. And I was stunned to speechlessness.

When Ivy Trove opened the door, I don't know how

my dad managed to control his facial features, such was the impact, but he did, managing a mask of polite indifference as if he hadn't noticed anything unusual. She was obviously rushing, having quickly changed into a plain black dress after the early morning chores, and was just putting her apron back on; but she smiled and the effect was electric. There was something about her above and beyond the physical that even now I struggle to explain. She had the kind of looks I now know aren't rare in certain parts of Cornwall and South Wales, but I'll try to do her justice. A golden, exotic-looking woman, she had luxuriant, glossy black hair, level brows, emerald green eyes, and fine-cut bone structure with a distinctive high-bridged nose. There was that je-ne-sais-quoi though, too. What was it? A deep, quiet confidence, a knowing, a mesmeric aura. I saw her then, through the eyes of a ten-year-old child, as an Egyptian queen.

"Say hello, Enys! And say thank you for all the pound notes you've received. Especially when we know how Auntie Ivy can't afford it."

The sparring between them was apparently legendary, but there it was – Round One to my mother – Ivy depicted as a poor country bumpkin while we were sophisticated Londoners – a card played, picked up seamlessly as if neither had ever left the gaming table.

We sat down in the kitchen while Ivy made tea and called Beatrice downstairs.

"George will be back soon," she said, in that warm, buttery brogue that's rarely heard these days. "He'm just finishing off outside."

Dad cleared his throat. "It's sad we have to meet for the first time on an occasion such as this."

"'Tis that," Ivy agreed, stirring the teapot. Stirring and stirring, ebony hair coiled high in a beehive on top of her head.

She set the pot on the table just as Beatrice burst in, all swinging dark hair and a pelmet of a mini skirt. Long, long legs, clad in white lacy tights. The longest I'd ever seen, like a colt.

"And who'd have thought your grandmother would have gone quite so suddenly, Josie? Overnight. Poor thing, suffered awful bad in the end with that crooked spine of hers. Got worse with age like her mother. Painful in the end, it was. Poor old lovely."

***

CHAPTER FOUR

Round two, it seemed, had gone to Ivy Trove.

My mother looked as if she'd just been smacked in the face with a pan. Any attempt to dull the shock would have been fruitless. She stared at the bare kitchen wall for what seemed like an eternity, the only sound the clock in the hall ticking methodically on.

Eventually, Ivy said, "Forgive me, I can't remember, do you take milk in your tea, Josie? Bea, pass the sugar to Auntie Josie."

My mother pushed her cup forwards. Thanks were muttered, and then, avoiding looking at anyone in particular, she grabbed hold of the carrier bags we'd brought. "Oh, while I remember, these are your Christmas presents. Just a few luxuries and whatnot – sort of things you can't get out here, I expect."

Ivy smiled. "Thank you. I've got yours upstairs. Bea, will you go and get them?"

"No, don't worry about that now," said my mother. "I'll pick them up later."

The teacup rattled in the saucer as she lifted it to her lips, Dad's incredulous stare boring into the side of her face. As mine was. Every nerve and sinew in her body had tightened to snapping point. You could feel the tension, hear your own heartbeat. And I'd never seen my dad like that before, either; he sat there stunned, not knowing what to say, how to be, slightly paler than when he came in.

And who'd have thought your grandmother would have gone quite so suddenly?

Any subsequent words exchanged by the adults bore almost no relevance to the ones needed. They were talking about the weather, about a storm expected from the North East and the possibility of snow. I'd been desperate to ask what Ivy meant, but one bullet-hard glance from my mother was enough. I thought Ivy had made a mistake. Why would she say Great Aunt Mary was my mother's grandmother? If my mother and Ivy were sisters, didn't they share the same grandparents?

She'm not my sister…

My mind was firing like an overloaded circuit board and I'm sure Dad's was, too. Because if what Ivy said was true, then my mother had lied. Lied to all of us. Lied to my dad. For years. He was shocked, anyone could see. And if Mary was her grandma, how come she'd been brought up at the farm and not at Gorse Bank House? The village women had called her Josie Trewhella. It didn't make sense and the questions were queuing up, even as Mum and Ivy moved swiftly on to discuss the hymns chosen for the funeral, as if one of them hadn't just handed a ticking time bomb to the other.

My dad, I thought, would wait until we were alone to confront her. Besides, there was a funeral to go to, and then refreshments at the village hall. I pictured the assembly room tables, could almost hear the chairs scraping across the parquet floor, smell the pastries and tang of sherry; and sensed the fractious aura surrounding my mother would only worsen. She'd been polite but curt earlier when talking to the village women, and I could well imagine the afternoon would be an endurance test for her. And me.

"The girls don't need to go, do they?" Ivy said to my dad. "No need to put them through the horrors of a funeral, not at their age."

Dad nodded, and the motion was carried before my mother had a chance to object.

"They'll be quite all right here. It'll be nice they can play together. Besides, I need Bea to keep an eye on the pups."

Looking back now, I can see that was the point at which my mother started to lose her grip, as if she'd known this was coming but had no idea how to stop it. She looked from Beatrice to me, then over at Dad, eyebrows raised. He barely met her eyes. Round three to Ivy, maybe? Best of three, or more to come?

My mother's intuition, however, was certainly on the money – it was a major mistake leaving me with Beatrice and she knew it would be, but what could she have done? It was achieved so smoothly, so easily, you could almost believe the whole thing was meant to be. I was certainly never the same again after spending a few hours with Beatrice.

In the living room, the embers of the fire were glowing hot and red, a warm and comforting contrast to the squally rain now sheeting off the moors; and after the adults had gone, we sat down on the rug by the hearth. She had hold of a pack of playing cards and began to shuffle them.

"Do you know how to play rummy?"

She was older than me and came across as aloof, self-contained. But there were sly, mischievous glances, too, green eyes flashing, glinting, dancing. Oh, she'd been bursting to tell me what she knew.

I nodded. "Yes, a bit. I've played it maybe once. Possibly twice."

"That be something, then."

Silently, she began to deal the cards.

"What are you having for Christmas?" I asked.

"A Decca record player. And Elvis Presley's new single. You?"

I shrugged, can remember feeling embarrassed about having asked for a hamster. They had dogs there – collies in the straw-filled barn with a litter of pups to give away – and horses too, animals being part of their daily life. It seemed so homely at the farm, so timeless and settled, with its sturdy Welsh dresser, the old grandfather clock ticking in the hall, and the aroma of home-baked bread. She made me feel… oh, I don't know, odd about myself, displaced and somehow babyish, less sure of who I was.

We had a game of rummy pretty much without speaking, followed by cat's cradle, and then she decided to teach me poker. Did I have any money?

I nodded.

Up to then we hadn't said much, but she was watching me. Covertly. My mind kept flicking back to what Auntie Ivy had said about Great Aunt Mary with the crooked spine.

But of course, I had no idea what was coming.

"'Mad Mary', they used to call 'er round 'ere," she said eventually, as if she'd read my mind, and casual as you like. "Either 'Mad Mary' or 'The pisky witch.' She'd sit and look out of the round window at the top of the 'ouse you're in – you know, the one in the middle with the lead cross?"

"What? Yes."

I was agog. Suddenly Beatrice started to talk, and it was as if a locked door had opened. Why had Mary been called that, I wanted to know. And why did my mum and Ivy look so completely different? Maybe they were cousins if they weren't sisters? I was confused, sat frowning as information then poured out of Beatrice's mouth. Beatrice, who I'd always thought was my cousin, whose coltish endless legs stretched out on the hearth rug as she threw down another playing card, and then another, smiling with that teasing half smile she and her mother shared.

She'd tied her curtain of black hair back with a bobble, emerald eyes flashing. She didn't have the same fine bone structure Ivy had, inheriting softer, flatter features from her father, George; and nor did she have that golden sheen, an aura that made Ivy look as if she was lit from within, but she had the rest. Along with that nugget of hidden knowledge just bursting to pop out like a genie from a lamp.

I looked nothing like them. No one would ever guess we were even remotely related. But then I didn't look much like my mother, either. Everyone, especially Gran and Grandad back home, said I took after my father. We, the Quillers, had sandy hair, freckles and grey eyes. We were tall but not especially so – I certainly didn't have legs like Cousin Beatrice. But nor was I petite and somewhat bony, with ice-pale eyes like my mother...

"What's a pisky witch?"

"You not 'eard of piskies, then?"

I shook my head.

"They be what you'd call the little folk. You must've heard of fairies? They'm not a joke, Enys Quiller. You've to respect them or you'll regret it. Not to be messed with, the little people."

"I thought fairy stories were just... stories? Made up?"

She shook her head, solemnly, although the lights in her eyes were sparkling.

"There's a pisky well in the woods behind the mill. I'll take you. If you go there, you can be cured of anything, but you've to ask nice and never take anything away from it or you'll fall foul of the piskies, and you don't want to do that. They be greatly affeared for good reason. They'll steal your horses and bring them back in the morning fit for nothing. Then there be piskies on the moors. There's many a story of folk getting mazed up there late at night, walking round and round in circles 'til they fall flat down from exhaustion or go under a bog. Pisky-led, they call it. 'Tis what 'appens to travelling tailors and other blow-ins, they just..." She paused for full effect. "Vanish."

Shrugging, she put down another card. "Stick."

"So piskies are like Will o' the Wisps, then?"

"No, much worse. If you don't end up dead, you become a pisky yourself and no one will know what happened to you, either. You'd just disappear forever or come back mazed and mad. You'd never go 'ome again, Enys."

I realise now her eyes were laughing, but at the time I was a bit scared.

"So what's a pisky witch, then?'

"Means those that talk to the little people. Mad as a March hare, your great grandmother was, Enys Quiller."

I nodded.

"With her pale, watery, close-together eyes." Between thumb and forefinger, she demonstrated an inch at best.

"Nearly crossed. Like she be looking at a jasper settling on the bridge."

There was a brief lull while that last sentence settled, and then she said, "Your mum came down 'ere for the money, you know, or she'd never 'ave come back. I reckon she must have known all along Mad Mary was her grandmother."

Oh, no! I shook my head. That my mother had been shocked the day she took the phone call, I was certain. She hadn't known. I could clearly remember the look on her face. If she knew, then she would have expected the inheritance. But it was a huge shock. It was!

To be honest, I didn't like the way things were going by then, with the talk of madness, witchcraft, crooked spines, and the old woman being my great-grandmother and most definitely not Beatrice's. I bit my lip, feeling un-armed, and unprepared for what might come next. Because Beatrice clearly hadn't finished.

"She wouldn't even have come to the funeral if she wasn't getting the 'ouse and you knows it. Has she ever had a good word to say for the place? Vowed never to set foot 'ere again, my mum said."

I didn't know what to think, and floundering, confused, focussed instead on an old sepia photograph propped up on the sideboard. Framed in silver, it was on a lace cloth, a brass paraffin lamp behind. The subject, a young woman, was posing with a small child on her lap, and wore a high-necked ruffled blouse with a bead necklace. Glossy black hair was piled high on her head, tendrils curling around an exquisitely fine-boned face. I'd seen her before – that was Auntie Ivy, except in Victorian dress. The child, two years old or thereabouts, stared confidently at the camera. Stocky, he had the same cutglass bone structure as his mother, but his eyes were chestnut brown and widely set, ticking up slightly at the outer corners along with his smile. I wanted to ask… Who? Another cousin?

But Beatrice, by then, was warming, to her theme. "Yes, so you see, your great-grandmother, Mad Mary, went round these 'ere lanes mumbling to 'erself. We all seen her. Ain't a secret. Talking to the little people. Had devil rituals in them pisky woods, lots of horses went sick and babies died from coughing. No one liked to cross her path and if she passed their doors, they'd put salt down. Went mad up at that big house in the end. You wouldn't catch me living there – not with her old skeleton bones rattling round them rooms, tap-tap-tapping along the floorboards with 'er stick. You'll hear 'er ghost now she's gone, I expect, in the dead of night, haunting the 'ouse like her mother before her. It was always haunted, that house. Been haunted for years and years and years. No one wanted to work there and that's why it be so cold and dirty. My mother wouldn't set foot in there. She didn't want to go up the drive to leave the key the other day. They say even the undertakers didn't want to go in to take her body out."

There was a pause.

"So then," she said, "there's something for you to think about."

I just sat there staring and staring at that old photo, blinking rapidly. Perhaps after a while, she regretted what she'd said and felt sorry for me, a child after all, of just ten. She'd been laughing, playing cards, winning all the games against a much younger player – well, two years younger but the gap seemed hugely wider – when suddenly her expression softened and she leaned over to touch my arm.

"You want to know who she is in that photograph, don't you? That be *my* mother's great-grandma, Tamara. Isn't she beautiful?"

I nodded.

"Funny your mother grew up here and not at the big haunted house, isn't it? Funny she called my mother her sister and never told you or your dad. I wonder why that is?"

I shrugged, trying not to cry.

"Oh, poor Enys. Probably you and your parents will want to leave now and go back up along." She indicated with a jerk of her head, the rest of the country. "But if you really want to know what happened in that house, because something really bad most definitely did, and that be why it's haunted and Mary went mad, then I dare say when the Droll Teller comes on Christmas Day, he might tell you."

My eyes widened as yet another thud of previously unknown information landed.

Something really bad happened? Droll Teller?

"And thing is, see, I'd be glad if you told me dreckly, what the real story is, because he's the only one who'll know. And in accordance with tradition and what is honourable, the droll teller only tells the new owner of a house the history. He'll never gossip outside of it. So, if your mother owns the house, he would tell her what went on, see?"

I nodded.

"And then you could tell me."

"What if he doesn't come?"

"Oh, he'll come. New owner. So, don't lose the chance. This all be on your shoulders now, Enys Quiller. So, make sure to ask him, won't you? When he says story or song? Say 'Story'!"

***

CHAPTER FIVE

Beatrice's fount of knowledge ran dry so abruptly it left me reeling. I'd been fully primed to hear what terrible thing had happened in the house, only to realise she didn't actually know, except everyone was terrified and nothing on earth would persuade them to spend a night there. But there was something else disturbing me too, that went unacknowledged at the time, but which turned out to be highly significant a few days later when it came to determining my own behaviour.

You see, while Beatrice was confident about who she was and where she belonged, I, Enys Quiller of Camden, had been cut suddenly adrift, the rope to my previous, clearly dull and slightly shameful identity, hacked as surely as a dinghy from a quay. I think I wanted to be Beatrice. I yearned to have what she had, to wake up and taste the salty sea frets on the air, to see the stone circle eternally silhouetted against a backdrop of wild moorland, to ride horses, go to the beach, look after puppies in the barn… I loved it already. And although I didn't look like Ivy and Beatrice, had never been there before, I had an almost painful need to stay, to belong, and already it had the power to make me cry. I didn't want to go home, couldn't bear to leave, and I think it was possibly that, the chance to please, to belong, which at least temporarily blinded me to the fear of what was to come.

I wanted to know more about the mysterious droll teller, who he was and when he would call. It seemed to me that so much rested on his visit, and that part at least, Beatrice knew all about.

"Oh, it be a well-known tradition round here," she said, going on to explain how storytellers and fiddlers, also known as scrapers, would gather crowds in market squares and inns, but also visit farms and big houses, especially at Christmas.

"Would have been good in long, bleak winters to have a bit of entertainment, wouldn't it? We have a barn dance for everyone here at the farm, and all the fiddlers come from miles about. That be on Christmas Day at six o'clock, so I expect as there's a new owner in the village, he'll turn up this year. I never seen him, mind. Do you want a bite to eat? They'll be back soon. I'm supposed to get things ready."

I followed her into the kitchen and she filled the kettle, setting it on the range in the inglenook. The room was heady with the aroma of yeast and sweet spices, and outside the window chickens clucked and squawked in the yard, scooting about in the wind. I thought about our small kitchen back in London, one I'd been perfectly happy with until then, comparing theirs with our yellow Formica cupboards, the pull-out table cramped in the corner by the frosted glass partition, and its view of the railway tracks.

"Mum left beef sandwiches and apple cake. So, you've not heard about the fiddlers and droll tellers, then?"

I shook my head.

She shook hers in disbelief. "What they do is play tunes and tell stories of how it used to be in the olden days, so our history doesn't die out – all the tales of rival lovers, murders, giants and mermaids, those who didn't pay heed to the little people, knockers in the tin mines, and smugglers and so on. And in return they're given a meal and a bed for the night. That's how I know so much, see? Anyhow, they come here at guldize and again on Christmas Day. 'Tis a great night, a big feast, and we're famous for it. Very exciting."

I sat at the long wooden table watching her slice and butter the apple cake.

"But like I said, there's an old man who allegedly visits all new dwellers, and that's special, a rare thing, and it never, ever doesn't happen, so mark my words he will come. If your mother lets him in, that is!" She paused to look at me, making sure I fully understood the implication. "So, that's something for ee to consider. Anyway," she continued buttering, "he's the one who'll have the story. About what went on afore your great-grandmother's time. Thing is, you never know, do you? What you'll find out? I bet Mad Mary knew, though. She must have done. I bet he told her when she took over the 'ouse." Her eyes widened. "That's it! I bet the droll teller told 'er. Probably what sent her mad, I never thought of that..."

A creeping unease settled on me then, as all she was saying gradually sank in. Something very frightening must have sent the old lady mad, and the prospect of actually seeing a ghost, a horrific apparition from unseen realms while I lay alone in bed, was beginning to loom over me, to become real. Beatrice went on and on about it, too – embellishing accounts of what she'd heard from those who'd worked in the house and never would again, about doors creaking open in the dead of night, candles being blown clean out and a mirror dropping off its hook on the wall. And as such, it was the first thing I blurted out when my mother, white around the gills, blew back in from the funeral sharp and prematurely, with my dad in tow.

"No," she said, clattering around with cups and cutlery. "There is absolutely no such thing as ghosts. Whatever have you been filling this child's head with, Beatrice?"

Bea was smiling in that same enigmatic way her mother did.

"Made me want to slap her," Mum said afterwards, as we walked briskly back up the hill.

The low, watery sun had dropped into a hazy horizon, and a cold sea mist had drifted inland, covering the landscape in an ethereal veil, incrementally blotting out the fields, hedgerows and woodland. It was foggy and damp, the wind spitting rain, our footsteps overly loud on the lane, breath panting. It had been a wrench to leave the warm, firelit glow of the farmhouse kitchen, and I was still thinking about it when we crossed the threshold onto the drive. And only then did my fears surface. As we neared the house, the image Beatrice had portrayed of Mad Mary gazing out of the round window rushed back. Immediately, I looked up, half expecting to catch sight of a ghostly face.

There was no one there.

Been haunted for years and years and years... My mother wouldn't set foot in that house...

Dad rooted in his pocket for the key, and we were shivering, hustling to pile inside, when the door swung open.

The contrast was striking and I'll not forget it, from the homely kitchen that smelled of cakes, to Gorse Bank House that smelled of... We all breathed it in... the unmistakeable odour of mildew that wafted down the icy hallway.

"It'd freeze the balls off a brass monkey in here," Dad said. "Keep your coats on 'til I get a fire going."

"Snow's coming," my mother said.

"Didn't think you got snow down here?"

"On high ground, yes. Listen, while you light a fire, I'll get a bed made up for Enys and do the hot water bottles. It's going to freeze tonight. Enys, go and find your navy sweater then come and help me in the kitchen."

I was torn. On the one hand, I was desperate to relate what Beatrice had said, to blurt out all I knew. But then again, remembering Beatrice's words, it might be best not to forewarn them about the droll teller. What if my mother decided not to let him in?

No, his visit had to catch her by surprise. My mother wasn't going to disclose anything, was she? Maybe she didn't know anything?

Thing is, you never know, do you? What you'll find out?

Maybe sometimes the things you desperately want to know might be better not known? Because once you've got that story, those images, that knowledge, it's yours, lodged in your head, and you can't ever give it back. Recreated by its new host, the story once again becomes real, it grows and grows, becoming stronger, muscling in on the direction of a new life, altering choices and perspectives.

But I was a child burning with curiosity and had no thought of consequences. I was the kind of girl who was entranced by secret gardens, doors in the backs of wardrobes, and the magical kingdoms beyond. And Beatrice Trove had opened a door I'd willingly wandered through. I suppose I wanted to be part of it all so badly, to be the one who could report back with that one hidden kernel of information that only I could find, a valuable and precious jewel that would make her like me, accept me, be grateful to me…

And so, that night the haunting was mine and mine alone. I could tell my parents nothing. Not yet. Not until the droll teller had been.

You'll hear 'er ghost now she's gone, I expect, in the dead of night, haunting the 'ouse like her mother before her... tap-tap-tapping with her stick…

***

CHAPTER SIX

That night was the first time I slept alone. There were three bedrooms at the front, and the one with the round window was in between mine and the one my parents shared, our collective view being the lane, a silvery moon-lit ribbon leading up to the moors.

It was not, however, the tap-tap-tapping of an old lady's walking stick that woke me in the early hours. Initially, I thought it was my mother nudging open the door, checking up on me. Ever since we'd returned from the funeral, she'd been watching me constantly –furtively and secretively – but definitely, constantly, watching. She never had before.

"So, what else did Beatrice Trove tell you, then?"

The question had caught me off guard earlier that evening, although deep down I was aware trouble was brewing. We'd been sitting by the fire in the lounge. It shone in red gleams around the inglenook and flickered around the walls, picking out gilt-edged paintings of bucolic scenes, and fussy ornaments in cabinets. The warm glow reached the ceiling, but left in shadow the hallway and the rest of the ground floor, where Dad was washing up in the kitchen. And so there we were, alone together, her words hanging between us.

Up until then we'd been busy, trying to make the house more homely, deciding which rooms were needed and closing off the rest. It seemed vast to me, a palace with high ceilings inset with intricate plasterwork, ornate coving, and long sash windows that rattled and whistled in the wind. There was a fireplace in every room upstairs and down, even the bathrooms. The room with the round window upstairs had certainly been one of the ones closed off. Piled high with junk, there'd been an old-fashioned chest obscuring the fireplace, and stacked against walls peeling with faded green wallpaper, there were chairs and boxes, a cradle, an ancient perambulator, and a sewing machine. And beneath the window was a window seat, maybe two feet deep, with a faded, frayed golden cushion on top. That's all I saw in what was the briefest of glimpses.

"We'll have to pay someone to come and clear all that away," Dad said, pulling the door shut again.

"What do you reckon it was, Jimmy – a nursery?"

"Maybe. Or a sewing room?"

To the rear of the house, adjacent to the lounge and overlooking a garden that swept all the way down to the river, was a generously proportioned Victorian kitchen. From what I can remember, it had a walk-in pantry, a big kitchen table, several freestanding dressers weighted with crockery, and a cast iron range with a wooden drying rack strung from the ceiling. Out back was a scullery, with a Belfast sink, washing machine and mangle, then another door into a corridor leading to an outside lavatory and the coal cellar. It could, without doubt, have been a beautiful family home, but had simply, as my parents said, been left to rack and ruin.

"You'd think she'd have got someone in," Dad said, opening a door to further ground floor rooms. "Look at the state of it!"

Clearly, they'd once been used as bedrooms, but now wallpaper stained with damp was peeling off the walls. It had slipped down in folds, pulling with it crumbling plaster, sliding slowly, incrementally, to the floor.

We'd discovered furred spores growing inside the pantry, and much of the paintwork at the back of the house was black with mould; and if you pressed on the window frames your finger went straight through. The pipes cranked and juddered, the floorboards were soft, the whole house was alive with the sound of ticking, scuttling and scratching. And even to this day I've never seen spiders as big or as bold. The cobwebs didn't simply brush away. Tough as fishnets, they had to be prised off. Those great, brown, hairy spiders lay in wait, spread-eagled across the walls, blending in with shadows, patterns and stains; they hid behind hinges and under doorways, lurking. Even my dad baulked once or twice. I'd never heard him swear before. Well, not like that. And although the house had electricity the lights were dim, as if you'd put sunglasses on, the gloom never truly lifting. So those things, those gigantic spiders, when you grappled for a light switch, could really catch you out.

Anyway, we'd just had supper when, with Dad in the kitchen, I'd found myself alone with my mother. The room, as I recall, was lit only by the glow of the fire, the darkness preferable to the somewhat jaundiced lighting from the central pendant and, that evening in particular, a blessing. It has always been my nature to share all I knew with anyone who asked, but there I was, saddled with the tricky business of concealing pretty much everything I'd just learned from the one person who I wasn't supposed to keep secrets from.

She was staring at me, waiting. And the longer the moment stretched, the more awkward it became. She had to be told something. But what? I was grateful for the flames to look into, as I stumbled through a psychological minefield of potentially explosive information. I'm pretty sure that what I chose to tell her she already knew – tales of piskies and travelling tailors vanishing in the bogs.

"Oh, and then we talked about pop groups and Christmas. She's having a record player."

"And that was all, was it?"

I nodded.

"So why did you ask if I believed in ghosts the minute we got back from the funeral? You've never asked about anything like that before, so it must have come from Beatrice. She'm a piece of work that one, just like her mother. Grinning like the cat that got the cream."

I shrugged.

"Don't lie to me, Enys."

I had that hot feeling inside and my heart began to speed up.

"She was just trying to scare me, I think."

My mother's eyes were lasers. "So what did she say to you, Enys?"

"Nothing much. She just said Great Aunt Mary would haunt the house, that's all. With her being dead… that all dead people do that… or, you know… stuff like that…"

Mum switched her attention back to the flames and my words tailed away, sounding as lame to my ears as they must have been to hers. She didn't believe me. I didn't believe me. I longed to off-load all that weighed so heavily on my mind, to receive reassuring explanations in return, but couldn't. She might stop the droll teller from speaking, if she had a secret to keep, from Ivy, from my dad, from me...

Funny she called my mother her sister and never told you or your dad. I wonder why that is?

And so, for the first time ever, I couldn't trust my mother.

And she couldn't trust me.

Dad was still in the kitchen, the sound of clattering crockery coming from down the hall, when suddenly her head jerked up.

"Enys, once and for all there's no such thing as ghosts. It's all made-up nonsense, do you hear? Just like all the other stories round here, it's tittle-tattle. Beatrice Trove has been trying to frighten you like you said yourself, and she should be downright ashamed. She was laughing at you, wasn't she? I saw her laughing like a malicious pisky. And you've got to sleep in your own room tonight as well, so you'd best put all that poppycock right out of your head or you won't sleep a wink."

I nodded, wanting desperately to believe her. "But what about the spiders? I can't sleep alone – what if one runs onto the bed?"

"Stop it now, Enys. I've vacuumed in there myself, every nook and cranny, and the bed's got fresh, clean sheets on. They can't hurt you, anyway."

"A girl at school said they bite, and someone said they can burrow into your ear and get into the brain. A woman had one in her hair, it laid eggs, and that was in the papers. Please can I sleep with you and Dad tonight? Please? Just one more time–"

But I knew and she knew, I'm sure of it, what was really worrying me. And it was the same thing worrying her, although I didn't know that at the time. She just looked me in the eyes when she tucked me into bed that night, and the words that came out were like a jug of iced water pouring down the spine.

"Enys, one more thing. If I ever find out there's something you didn't tell me that you should have, I will never forgive you, do you understand?"

As the door closed behind her, the fear of her wrath briefly outstripped the fear of any ghostly apparitions. However, it was not, as I said, the ghostly tap-tap-tapping of an old lady's walking stick that woke me up that night. Nor was it my mother checking in on me. Rather, it had been water, the sound of someone splashing water. I must have fallen into a deep sleep because the jolt awake was like an electric shock. I'd been awakened suddenly and sharply.

I lay absolutely motionless in the deep, velvety darkness, ears straining into the silence, acutely aware of each creak and sigh of the house.

Someone had splashed water close by, as if in the same room.

My whole body thumped with each heartbeat.

That's probably what sent her insane, see, like her mother before her – the hauntings. Been haunted for years and years and years... My mother wouldn't set foot in that house...

And then, unbidden, the image flashed up of old Mary staring out of the window in that cluttered room on the other side of the wall. And it would not go. There she would be on the faded gold cushion, looking through the glass with the iron cross, at the frosty lane winding up to the moors, at the stone circle silhouetted against the night sky. Was she there now as she had been in life? Why had she sat there? Watching or waiting for what? Or who?

Everyone had seen her, Beatrice said… always looking out… every day…

I stared until my eyes teared up, at that blank wall. The only gleam of light came from a thin strip beneath the doorway to the landing, maybe a lamp on in my parents' room, just enough to see the outline of the washstand in the far corner, and a cumbersome walnut wardrobe crammed with old dresses and fur stoles, the arm of one flowery blouse trapped in the door.

It was all right, I reassured myself, Mum and Dad were just a few yards away, they had a lamp on, ghost stories were nonsense, just tittle-tattle from Beatrice, a cat who got the cream, laughing at me, trying to scare me. I told myself this over and over, and had just started to breathe again, to relax ever so slightly and sink back into sleep, when there came a sharp, loud and most definite click. Like that of a key turning in a lock. And no sooner had I registered that a door had creaked open, when a shadow dimmed the strip of light beneath the door.

Horrified, I strained to hear. I was on full alert for the tap-tap-tapping of a stick. Mad Mary was coming, Mad Mary was coming! She'd come out of the room with the round window. My heart catapulted. It was all true. There were ghosts! Everyone had lied. Both parents had lied! And now something was about to spring on my appalled senses, some monstrous dweller standing on the threshold. A freezing possession took hold of me then, a sickly thudding in my chest, and my hair seemed to rise out of the follicles. Someone was there, just standing outside my door!

"Mum?"

No answer.

"Mum? Dad?"

It was then the whispering started, faintly, becoming more insistent, a top note above the sound of the wind soughing in the trees, around the windows and down the chimneys. And it was getting louder.

"Enys!" It sounded like, "Enys!"

She was whispering my name, over and over and over. Mad Mary was standing outside the door… about to push the door open…

"Dad! Dad!"

And then the sulphur yellow of the landing light came on, and he was there.

"What is it, Enys? Only it's two in the morning."

"It's Mad Mary, she's here." My voice was breaking, and even as I told him I knew he didn't believe me. I couldn't breathe properly. "She got out… she… was there on the landing–"

He sounded tired beyond measure, his voice pleading. "No, Enys. There are no ghosts. You've had your head filled with absolute nonsense."

He spent a while reassuring me. And I know I'd felt, for a short time, comforted that all was normal, that whatever I thought I'd heard could be explained by what had been said that day, all mixed in with dreams. Just like he said. That's how the brain worked, he explained – it tried to make sense of things. He was only surprised I hadn't dreamt of piskies threading little stirrups into the manes of horses, before galloping across the moors. I'd smiled at that, promised him I'd be okay. Soon be morning. Soon be Christmas, two days to go, and then we'd be going home again. It was an old house, unfamiliar, that was all.

But after the door was pulled softly shut again, I heard it quite distinctly and without any doubt whatsoever: a soft rustling sound like some small silk thing blown in a breeze. Right next to my face.

***

Chapter Seven

Next day, Saturday, was the day before Christmas Eve. We went to Gulston, a town by the estuary that had steep cobbled streets weaving up from the quayside, and an openair market. The mist had been slow to lift and when the pale sun came through it was cold, and an icy chill blew off water that was battleship grey, gulls screeching over a jetty of rough boulders and beams dripping with seaweed.

Dad and I were wandering around the market stalls looking for tinsel, fairy lights, and glitter for the pine cones we planned to collect, while my mother disappeared on a secret shopping mission. There was an air of excitement, people were in high spirits, the mood more of a drunken cheer as lunchtime neared. And outside the Ship Inn a fiddler was playing Christmas tunes. As we passed I caught his eye, looking at him with a curiosity I probably wouldn't have done before meeting Beatrice. These were the people who knew the secrets, kept the old tales alive, the hidden knowledge... He was busy nodding thanks to those throwing coins into his hat, but in that fleeting glance I fancied we connected in some way, that there was an acknowledgement. His bright, currant eyes met mine and held, time suspended, the moment feeling like a marker, an omen, significant somehow.

My dad was telling me we needed another bottle of

sherry or Father Christmas wouldn't come, and as the old man picked up his violin again, I was already drifting away, smiling. Dad trod gently with the Santa illusion; I'll give him that. I wasn't quite ready to grow up, and looking back I can see how he tried to protect that, to prolong my childhood as best he could during those last few days. We had a magical morning, the smell of hot pasties wafting on the brisk sea air so tantalising that we wolfed them down, sitting on a wall in the car park before setting back. It wasn't far – ten minutes.

That day was blissful, prized now, a shimmering gold sovereign at the bottom of a deep and murky well. Still there. But you don't see it unless you sit for the longest time, and the day is a clear one, the light at just the right angle.

Someone had once loved Gorse Bank House, you could tell. They'd loved the garden, too: that morning we found, in the died-back winter debris, miniature carvings of owls and pheasants, a fountain coated in lichen, and then a stone arch, gothic style, set into the bordering wall, beyond it fields and woodland. Someone had tucked a small, smooth, amber-coloured stone into a gap and I took it out, mildly curious, before putting it back. There was so much to explore, including several separate, sheltered garden enclosures, each leading off from the other – one with a small patio which had an apple tree planted in the middle, another with a sundial, and a rusty wrought iron table with a discarded trowel on top. It was almost as if another family had only just left; that the house, the garden, the whole scene, had been waiting patiently for a new cast, a new story. I ran around long after Dad had gone inside, discovering more hidden gems - a sculpted tortoise, a birdbath, more smooth stones tucked into crevices... The frosty air was scented with pine, my face chilled to ice as the temperature plummeted, the last glorious moments of that morning spent in innocent childhood treasured and held onto.

Afterwards, we all set to work thoroughly cleaning the parts of the house we'd be using, washing down walls, scrubbing cupboards and cleaning windows. My mother said the mould would make us ill, the damp would cause pneumonia, and besides, it wasn't good enough for Christmas, decorations couldn't disguise a pigsty. It was such a good day and one I remember well, throwing myself into the allotted tasks, and periodically I forgot altogether about the other things, about the night before, so that when I remembered, the horror washed over me afresh in a shivery sweat, in sickly waves.

Could the sound of splashing water that woke me have been one parent or the other in the bathroom? Could it? Was it possible? The small voice inside me said, yes, that was likely the case. But it had sounded much closer than the bathroom, in the same room in fact, a few feet away from my head. And there'd been some other sound too, although I couldn't yet say what that was. There had also been the click of a key in a lock, and the shadow under the door... and then, worst of all, the icy breeze that blew on my face after Dad had left. I kept busy anyway, asking for more things to do, and by the time I was rolling pine cones in glitter at the kitchen table, I'd almost succeeded in forgetting. Almost.

It wouldn't happen again. It was a dream, just a bad dream.

Dusk had fallen by four o'clock, the western sky a haze

of blush pink; and the house, by then, was considerably cleaner and more homely, a fire in the inglenook taking the chill off the lounge. The food wasn't good in those days, I've bad memories of liver and onions, suet puddings and the like, but Mum liked her jacket potatoes with cheese, and they did nicely in the range. And while those were cooking, we decorated the downstairs with freshly cut glossy, spiky sprigs of holly with red berries, tinsel and pine cones. We put up the cards we'd brought from home, strung fairy lights around the mirror over the hearth, and then had supper by the fire.

"Not so bad, is it?" Dad said, his face aglow. "Bit more comfortable for a couple of days anyway, Josie."

"Mmmm…?"

The overriding memory of my mother, when I reflect on what she was like just before the story came out, was that she was distant. As if she'd accepted an inevitability, that there was nothing she could do, and had already floated away like a balloon into the ether. Neither of us could reach her. It was bewildering, she'd always been so dominant, so sure of herself, and pivotal – the one who decided everything. And Dad's natural ease and jollity whenever he took time off work, which he normally delighted in, seemed forced and awkward. Probably their façade was for my benefit. I imagine they'd said to each other to keep a lid on things, to let Enys have a nice Christmas, to wait until it was over.

"How about a game of Snakes and Ladders, everyone?" Dad suggested, rubbing his hands together just like Grandad Quiller did.

"It's upstairs. In one of the carrier bags," said Mum.

I could not be left alone with my mother again. "I'll get

it."

"No, Enys. Your dad will go. You stay here."

The second he left the room, it was as if she and I had never left our seats from the previous night. That's when I knew she hadn't finished with me, not by a long shot. I badly didn't want to be alone with her, and my whole body stiffened. Oh God, what was coming?

Upstairs, the floorboards creaked as Dad walked along the landing to the bathroom. Then the bathroom door clicked shut.

Her voice was a gunshot. "So, Enys, when are you going to tell me what Beatrice Trove really said yesterday? Or do I have to go down there and have it out with her?"

"Nothing! Nothing else. I told you everything."

"Just pisky tales and silliness about ghosts? You're absolutely sure about that?"

I nodded, hugging myself, avoiding looking at her.

"And you haven't spoken to your father about anything? Something you've forgotten to tell me?"

"No."

"Enys, there will be no Christmas presents this year for children who lie to their parents. Santa does get to know."

It was a gut punch. I'd never heard her say anything like that before. Never had she threatened to take away my Christmas presents. To this day I can recall the shock. Tears swam into my eyes.

"What?"

"Don't say, 'What?'"

She was glaring at me. It was as if in that moment she hated me, her face set so rigid it was no longer hers, the eyes stony. Dad's feet thundered overhead. Likely there was less than a minute before he'd be back. What did she want to know? What was she so worried about? How to please, to make her like me again… and yet conceal…?

"I–"

He called out from the kitchen, so close already we both jumped.

"Want a sherry, Josie?"

"Yes, thanks."

"Shan't be a tick!"

There was a *thwop* sound from the kitchen as he pulled out the cork.

"I'm waiting, Enys. You've got thirty seconds. Less."

I'd have to tell her something or she'd go marching down to see Beatrice and that would be unthinkable. Horrible. I was torn by indecision, unable to think clearly, not knowing what to do and blinded by panic.

"Just that… just that…" I couldn't meet her eyes for long, keeping my gaze determinedly on the flames, at how in the middle some were indigo and some lemony. "Just that my great-grandmother, auntie, grandmother, was mad. They all called her Mad Mary and that she had a crooked spine that got worse and worse with age until she was bent over double like a witch–"

"I see! Go on."

"And that she'll haunt the house like her own mother did, and that the hauntings had sent her mad, and she did devil things in the woods."

My mother's stare was unrelenting. It was as if an invisible probe had been thrown out, one now reeling in information against my will. She meant to glean every last drop, too.

"With piskies," I added.

"And?"

"She said you came back for the money or you wouldn't have come. That you hated the place and you knew Mad Mary was your grandmother all along. I said you didn't. But she said there was a story you weren't telling–"

"What story I'm not telling? What's that supposed to mean? What story?"

My heart was banging like a gong in my ears, pulsing in my throat, crashing inside my whole head. The words flew out then, without thought. "I don't know! Like, why you grew up with Ivy Trove at the farm. You don't look like her, not one bit. Why did you say she was your sister? Why didn't you live here, in this house? She said you knew!"

By the time Dad walked back in with two sherries and a board game, it was to a wall of stunned silence. My mother was as white as starched sheets.

"Everything all right?"

He handed her a glass and I noticed her hands were shaking. That, to me, was worse than anger – she looked scared, deeply unnerved.

Dad glanced at me and I saw the question in his eyes.

"Yes, we're absolutely fine," my mother said. "Enys has been telling me what Beatrice Trove's been saying, that's all. Anyway, let's have a game, shall we? Did you find it?"

I felt sick then, and somehow bereft. My orange squash tasted like chemicals, and even sprinkling the little blue bag of salt in the crisps did nothing to give them taste. Beatrice had been right: my mother was hiding something terrible – she hadn't denied or explained a thing! And it had a lot to do with Mad Mary. Here in this house. And now another night was coming.

As bedtime drew ever closer, the ghostly silken breeze

that had brushed my face the night before, again plagued my mind and I couldn't shake it. Desperately, I wanted more reassurance, that ghosts really didn't exist, and if they did they couldn't hurt you. I didn't dare ask them again, though. My mother barely looked at me, the sinews of her face taut, the atmosphere brittle. And an insidious chill had begun to shiver around our backs, stealing in from the corners of the room and the gloomy hallway beyond. The fire was dwindling too, weaker, the logs not really catching.

Finally, after three games of Snakes and Ladders, Mum spoke the words I'd been dreading all evening. "Go and get your bath now, Enys. Chop, chop! Christmas Eve tomorrow."

The jollity was forced, something none of us felt.

The house crawled with shadows. And it rattled just as Beatrice had said. It rattled like a bag of bones in a rocking, swaying carriage, as the wind began to pick up that night, shaking the window frames and doors.

I was put to bed, and downstairs the lounge door was firmly shut. And for a long time I lay listening to the whistling wind, and the living creaks and groans of the house, the shifting of tiles on the roof, and the incessant ticking, scuttling noises of creatures behind the walls. As tiredness washed over me, in came a backward sweep of memories, freshly jarring… and that's when I knew for sure the sound of splashing water that woke me the night before, hadn't come from the bathroom but from the washstand in the corner. My eyes were drawn to it, and the glint of the mirror above. There'd been something else, another sound, some other elusive thing that hadn't quite come to the surface yet…

One thing was certain - I must not, could not, go to

sleep. I waited on full alert until my parents had come upstairs, feeling safer when they were only two doors away. But even then I couldn't sleep, lying waiting instead, expecting to hear the click of a lock, for the strip of light under the door to dim. And then when the night claimed the blackness as its own, and there was only the howling wind battering the walls and shaking the windows, I closed my eyes tightly, and prayed.

"Please God, please! Don't let her come for me. Please don't let Mary get out of the room. Please don't let me go mad."

***

CHAPTER EIGHT

The face that appeared in the mirror struck a terror into me I would never forget. And God knows I tried. Nor did time diminish the memory. I only had to think of that night and her image would instantly reconjure, the details, the horror, every bit as vivid decades later, as it was then.

She wore a long white petticoat, the kind worn beneath a Victorian dress, and her black hair was loosely pinned up, falling in damp tendrils around a face pinched grey, her lips shrunken and shrivelled. She had the look of a living corpse, dead and yet not, because she was moving. It was the eyes, however, that were most disturbing, the expression as they met mine in the mirror – hot coals burning from within a ghastly mask – forever etched on my mind. The wild madness of her stare had cast around for the one she'd sensed watching. Then settled on me.

I had the briefest of warnings, less than a heartbeat, that she'd rush at me, slicing through my skin in a sheet of ice. A clammy coldness had spread all over my body, along with a roaring in my ears that persisted and wouldn't stop, long after I'd sprung back against the wall and screamed the house down; long after Dad had insisted again and again that ghosts did not exist, telling me the words I longed to believe, and a lamp had been brought in, the door wedged open with a chair… Long, long afterwards, even as dawn filtered through the darkness. Still I lay wide awake, rigid, alert and scared.

It's difficult to recall the specifics of what happened, because of the horror that temporarily blinded, deafened and paralysed me; but sometimes, if I can do so without that terrifying stare locking onto mine again – almost as if she'd crawled into my brain from that moment onwards and watched me from within – a few more details surface.

I must have eventually drifted off, probably relaxing just enough after Mum and Dad had gone to bed, only to be woken again shortly after. Certainly there was water, splashing water. My eyes had snapped open to see a figure at the washstand in the corner of the room. I'd been right, was my initial thought – that's where the sound had come from before! The woman had been scrubbing at her skin, furiously, obsessively so, vigorously attacking her hands and forearms with a nail brush, then plunging them back into the water. She was extremely agitated and impatient, working herself into a frenzy.

I'd lain there paralysed, breathing on hold, unable to believe the evidence of my own eyes. It was impossible, however, to look away – even though I knew, knew without any doubt whatsoever, that if I didn't, she would see me. And then what...? But I had no time, not a single second to react, to think, to move, to pray. The very moment I registered her existence, it seemed she registered mine. Her head jerked up and she stared into the mirror. Straight in. Stopping what she was doing as abruptly as if someone had crept into the room silently behind her, catching her in an illicit act. What had disturbed her? Who was there?

Her skin was haggard, blue-white, and coated in a greasy sheen. Sweating and shivering, she seemed feverish, one gravely ill. The apparition, in short, was enough to stop the heart of a grown man let alone a child, and that was before she abruptly swung around and glared at me with coal-black eyes full of fury and hate.

Was there anything else significant? Dear God, even now it's difficult to re-examine the details of that night, for fear of what it may recreate – the steel blade of fear, the panic of free-falling into nothingness, into blackness, into madness. And that's undoubtedly why it took so long before I could ask myself the necessary question: what, before I heard splashing water, had I heard? What had it been? Sobbing, muffled sobs… Yes, I think so. But what else, that elusive thing…? Eventually though, it did come to me. Laboured breathing, that's what it had been – wheeziness, gasping for air, like that of a far, far older woman.

Or a sick one?

With dawn on the horizon, I'd finally fallen asleep, straight into a lucid dream. It was not unpleasant, but nor did it dissipate on waking. In fact, even now I can recall every detail as if it happened yesterday. The woman in the dream had glossy ebony hair and jewel-green eyes, a high-bridged nose and sculpted cheekbones. Of course, when I thought about this many years later, I put it down to the photograph on Ivy Trove's sideboard, the resemblance to both Ivy and Beatrice unmistakeable. That kind of startling beauty was bound to stay with me, to form an enduring image that would feature in dreams. Except, not only do I remember it so clearly even to this day, but unlike the elusive, rapidly fading dreams I'd had before, and since, I lived it. I played a role. And my heart responded. I was absolutely, irrefutably involved. And for night after night, that dream replayed in exactly the same way, each time moving the story, if you will, a little further on.

She'd been sitting on a window seat, embroidering, from time to time glancing up and smiling – a lady in a high-necked, ruffled white blouse with a beaded necklace and a crocheted shawl around her shoulders. Behind her, the sky was deep azure and cloudless, and I knew it was a summer's day, that stooks of corn were ready to harvest, that miners and farmers alike lay spread-eagled on the grass after the day's work, dozing under a blistering late afternoon sun, that bees droned beneath the windows of the house and wild honeysuckle scented the air.

"Enys! Enys!"

Filling the window in a skirt that billowed large as a tent, she seemed content, dreamy, working away with needle and thread as she sat sideways on, alternately looking out of the window, then back over to me. The only difference between her and Ivy Trove to the eye, however, apart from the mode of dress, was the pallor of the skin. Where Ivy's was golden, this woman's was as grey-white as dingy linen, as waxy and translucent as death itself. Perhaps the dream had amalgamated Ivy's beauty with that of the ghost I'd seen? Dreams can be so strange, can't they?

And she may have been humming, singing, or breathing heavily, I couldn't say. She'd been happy though, anticipatory even, of that I'm certain, and most especially happy when she looked directly across the room at me, to where I lay sleeping…

"Enys! Enys!"

…as morning chased the shadows of dawn across the moors, gulls shrieked noisily over the fields…

… and Christmas Eve blew in.

Why was it summer?

I woke up disorientated. My bedroom was full of light, the air freezing, the sound of cups clattering downstairs. Then I remembered where I was. Oh, thank God!

I was so relieved that I leapt out of bed and flung open the curtains. The beauty of the scene was breath-taking. The fields and moors were white with frost, the view transformed overnight into an icy wonderland, a true Narnia; and with the aroma of toast and wood smoke in the air, I wanted to think only of one thing. And that was Christmas. It was almost Christmas Day. Pulling on my dressing gown, I bounded downstairs, already throwing off the terror of the night before like a wet cloak. When halfway down it hit me, hard as a cricket bat, with such force I had to stop and hold onto the banister.

The dream! The window behind the woman had been round. I'd been there, in that room, I know I had. I remember the wallpaper, too. Wallpaper that was deep, lustrous green, floral, and there was a rocking horse and a jack-in-the-box next to my bed... a bed that creaked, and swayed...

But that was not my room.

She used to sit and look out of that round window at the top of the 'ouse you're in now – you know, the one in the middle? You seen it, of course?"

***

CHAPTER NINE

However, that day matters took a dramatic turn of a more down-to-earth nature, and it certainly took my mind off the ghostly dreams, which I'd once again managed to persuade myself that's all they were.

My mother must have done some serious thinking. My dad doesn't do lies, you see? He's as straight as they come, gets hurt by those who try to take him for a fool. She knew that. And she knew full well what was coming as soon as Christmas was over. So, like I said, she'd been thinking.

"All right, I'll tell you what I know," she said.

It was later that day, and we were finishing lunch at a café with a panoramic view of the sea at Wraths Bay on the north coast. The waves were crashing onto the rocks below and occasionally spray hit the window so violently people screamed. The place was small, steamy, festooned with tinsel, and Christmas carols were playing on the radio. We'd had a long walk along the beach, heads down against a raw wind slanting off the Atlantic. The coastline is characterised by steep cliffs and jagged dark outcrops, and huge rolls of surf were racing in on the swell, roaring and thumping onto the shore. The wet sand shone gold that day, magnificent lines of breakers glinting in the wintry sun; and further in, close to the cliff face, were inky rock pools known as mermaids' glass. To the west side of the bay there was an arch of rock, a natural hydrophone that, when the wind was in a certain direction, sounded like a human sigh; or the death groans of drowning sailors, depending on the imagination or sensitivity of the listener.

Unlike Dad, I'd been transported again, willingly, carried away by the old tales my mother was telling us. I loved the salty taste of the air, the wild dunes with tufts of windswept grass, and the hypnotic hiss and roar of the ocean.

And earlier that morning I'd loved being on my own in the garden at Gorse Bank House, too – running freely down to the river, inhaling its sweet, cold freshness. It seemed to permeate the skin, made you feel clean inside, and I'd crouched down to watch it gush and chatter its way over stones glossy with ribbons of green, spraying crystals into the clear, bright sunlight. Dense firs sparkled with frost, there were crimson berries like jewels of blood amid forest foliage, secret gardens that seemed frozen in time; and high above stretched the iced-white fields, wild moors and the outline of the stone circle. I found it beautiful beyond expression and never wanted to leave, the pull was so strong. I could have stayed out there all day, but we had just one day to explore the coast. One day before Christmas.

Because of me, we couldn't go into The Mariner's Rest on the quayside – a Devon longhouse with white cob walls strewn with nets and anchors – and so we sat in the steamy café that was serving Christmas lunches. The table was brown Formica, the chips on my plate spotted with ketchup. Dad had been walking behind us all afternoon like a chaperone aunt, well behind, barely a word exchanged between him and my mother all day. I'd been aware, on some level, that they'd only spoken to me since breakfast and not each other, although not everything made sense. Of course, I realise now they hadn't been speaking to me at all. Anyway, they were nose to nose in the café, their emotions a rain cloud threatening to break any moment, an atmosphere at odds with the merriment around us.

I'd spiked a chip and tipped my head back to drop it down whole.

"Use your knife and fork, Enys!" my mother snapped.

Dad kept his eyes firmly fixed on her face. "Come on then, let's have it, Josie."

Her eyes flicked to me.

"She's had her head filled with all sorts from Beatrice already, you said it yourself, so you may as well tell us both. Whatever it is."

She'd stared out of the window at the ocean for so long that a knot began to form in my stomach. I had the feeling, and it turned out I was right because he confirmed it many years later, that he'd tried to talk to her already but she'd refused. Why? Because she had a secret to hide or because she was scared of the unknown? He'd had enough, anyway, had been asking himself if he could live with someone who'd deceived him for years; but more than anything he didn't understand why. All I knew was that it felt like a stand-off, kind of final, as if one of them was about to give up and could walk away… forever…

I pushed my plate away. Still can't stand the sight of ketchup.

"Come on then, what's the big secret? Okay, so Ivy isn't your real sister, that's obvious: you don't look anything like her, not even the faintest resemblance and you've said as much yourself. But, so what? What I want to know is why you ever said she was? And why did she sign herself as, 'Auntie Ivy' on the Christmas cards she sent to Enys? You don't have to be related to grow up together, there's no shame for either of–"

"I know."

"So, help me out, then! Did the Trewhellas adopt you? Although that wouldn't explain the birth certificate, would it, saying they're your parents? But we'll gloss over that for the moment and say these things happened, especially in wartime. So, Ivy's actually your stepsister, have I got that right?"

She said nothing.

"Look, obviously, you don't get on, but…" He reached for her hands, managing only to grasp her fingertips as she tried to pull away. "Josie, it doesn't matter to me that you're adopted, or that your genetic grandma was apparently suffering from some sort of mental illness. Maybe she was just lonely? Maybe with her daughter, or was it her son, killed in the war, she became depressed?"

There was a click in my mind, then. So, that was why Mary was always at the window – waiting for a child to come home from the First World War, but they never had? Or maybe a husband? Suddenly, it all seemed unbearably sad.

"We both love you and that's all that's important, Josie, surely?"

Her eyes gleamed with tears, then. But she blinked them away and didn't return the squeeze of the hands.

"I just don't get why you'd be so secretive about it. Being adopted and not getting on with your younger sister isn't exactly unheard of. I can perfectly understand why–"

"It's not that," she said, pulling her fingers out of his

grasp altogether. "You've got it all wrong. You're barking way up the wrong tree with all this. Just stop it, will you?" Again, her eyes flicked to me before she stared meaningfully at him again.

He frowned, took a breath, then tried a different tack. "Okay, well is it that Beatrice, somewhat gleefully by the sound of it, told Enys your heritage was madness and a degenerative condition–?"

He got no further.

"No, no and no. Look… just, no. It's not that."

"So, help me to understand then. Just tell me the truth, for Christ's sake! And then we can go home after Christmas, sell that place and never come back. Frankly, with house prices in London sky-rocketing, we could use the proceeds for a bigger one if you want, but you owe it to Enys even more than me, to tell us who you really are–"

"What? Who I really am?" She was looking at him pleadingly, silently begging him to stop.

He eyeballed her right back, not wavering. "Yes."

The afternoon light was already beginning to dim, heavy clouds massing on the horizon, suspended over the vast grey ocean. A wash of sleet spattered across the window. People were standing up, buttoning coats, the café getting ready to clear everything away and close up.

"Snow's coming," my mother said.

Dad looked like he was about to stand up, too.

"All right, then," she said, so faintly it was barely discernible. "All right…"

She closed her eyes and sighed. She must have thought she could breeze back to Hunters Combe, do her duty, call an estate agent after Christmas, and then we'd all go home much better off, her nursing days and the much complained about sluice room duty, a distant memory. Only it didn't work out that way. Truth has a way of coming out. And ghosts may not lie as silently and peacefully as some would like.

But even knowing she'd been adopted and the birth certificate untrue, she must have thought she could get away with telling only half the story - that the rest could be brushed aside with just enough to satisfy our curiosity? Or maybe she only knew half?

"I'll tell you what I know. But don't say I didn't warn you, though." She glanced at me. "Both of you. Are you ready for this, Enys?"

I nodded.

"All right. Well, I've not said anything in order to protect you. I didn't deem it proper you knew certain things, or ever needed to, but you want to know so that's as it is." She pursed her lips and then out it came.

"Right, well firstly, Trewhella Farm, where me and Ivy grew up, is not hers or mine. Nor was it the Trewhellas'. Mum and Dad were tenants and all that passed onto Ivy was the tenancy, the business, the livestock. That's why she needed George Trove or one like him and put herself about a–"

Dad sighed impatiently.

"They left her everything and me nothing, but I didn't know it was only the tenancy and not ownership of the farm and land. She let me think for all these years that it was. I never knew 'til now. I was so upset about it at the time, I didn't want to ever go back again or see Ivy's face. I'm sure you can understand that? How hurt I was to have been cast aside, that I didn't matter to anyone, that their Will contained absolutely nothing for me? Nothing.

"Anyway, after our mother died I stayed at the farm for the funeral. I was working at St Barts at the time, just before I met you, and Ivy was, I suppose, an angry, grief-stricken young woman, but she lashed out at me that day. There was just the two of us after everyone had gone home and she'd had a sherry or two, we both had, and that was when she blurted out that our mother had told her on her deathbed that I wasn't one of them, that I'd been an illegitimate baby from the village. And that was why I'd got nothing. I must be stupid not to be able to see how different I looked, how small and bony and pale… On and on she went. I upped and left soon as I could next morning, but before I did I told her not to repeat all that, not ever, not to anyone, because if there was even a shred of truth to it, then our parents had committed a crime. She was a bit more contrite by then, but agreed. It sounded as if they'd done a kind thing by taking in an unwanted child, and neither of us ought to turn that into a family disgrace. Besides, she'd got everything, hadn't she? Her a millionairess if she played her cards right. Me a pauper. What did she have to gain?

"So, I never said anything, Jimmy. Why would I? But I lost my roots that day, you see? I didn't belong anywhere anymore. Where, or who, had they got me from? I never even thought about Great Aunt Mary, she didn't feature in my life at all up to that point, and I didn't want her to, either. We had nothing to do with her, nothing. I thought she was a distant relative who was a bit of an embarrassment at best. I left anyway, and Ivy stayed. Ivy, who then became a lynchpin in the village, popular, the heart and soul, employing a lot of them, too.

"But it turned out the farm and everything else at

Hunters Combe, including all the cottages and the other farms, all the land, never actually belonged to any of the Trewhellas at all! The whole lot belongs with the Hamlyn estate. You'll recall the vicar's name at the funeral was Tom Hamlyn? They own it all, collect the rentals and so on, like old-fashioned tithes to this day, but I only found that out recently. Tom Hamlyn told me or I'd not have known even now. I made a chance remark about it being my turn to own something. She never told me, see? That sly piece let me think she owned it like she was lady of the manor."

"I see."

"Anyway, the adoption wasn't done through any authorities – that's why no one knew, including me – I was just handed over as a baby, and all that time everyone called me Josie Trewhella. Ivy told me after the funeral that Mary's daughter was my natural mother. She'd been barely out of her teens and died in childbirth. Apparently, Mary never got over it, so that's why I was given away, because Mary went to pieces. Everyone in the village knew. Everyone except me, and they only held their tongues out of respect for our parents."

I was trying to follow a whole new story by then, with an old lady so badly bereaved she'd lost her mind. But why, then, did she wait at the window as the villagers said?

My mother hadn't finished, though. "I don't know who my real father is either, Jimmy. That's the shame of it, see? In a small village like this, it was a very shameful thing and couldn't be allowed to get out. Ivy said he'd been a passing tailor on his way back to London. They'd all laughed behind my back. See? See now why I didn't want to talk about any of this? Why I felt it was best left."

Except the ghosts wouldn't lie still. Would they, Mum?

Dad nodded. "And that's it?"

"Isn't that enough? I thought I was the older sister at the farm, that my parents really were my parents and I'd inherit equally to my younger sister, then found out none of that was true and instead my grandma was the one everyone called a lunatic, a pisky witch, Mad Mary with the crooked spine. And I'd been given away and my birth certificate was fake but not to mention that! Now do you see why I was stunned when she just blurted it out like that –telling you and Enys that Mary wasn't a distant auntie after all, but my grandma. What must you think of me, Jimmy?"

"None of this is your fault. It's not even provable." Dad reached again for her hands and this time she didn't snatch them away.

"That's not all," she sniffed.

We waited while she got a handkerchief out of her handbag, clipped the bag shut again, and blew her nose.

"I only found this last bit out after speaking to Tom Hamlyn after the funeral, but Mad Mary really wasn't mad, you know? She had a bent spine that got worse over time, and also suffered from depression after her daughter's death, but she wasn't mad. In fact, he said the family was puzzled she hadn't used their usual solicitor, but, in his own words, slinked off to a new one to have her Last Will and Testament drafted. You saw Ivy thick with Vic Hamlyn at the church? Something's going on they don't like, but it seems Mary left all her documents, going back a century or more, with this new one, Lovelyn and Waterford in Gulston. The title deeds to Gorse Bank House had been bequeathed to her by her father, who was the local doctor. Now this is where it gets interesting: his name was Bray.

Tristan Bray. And he acquired the house by marrying a woman called Tamara Hamlyn – Mary's mother and my great-grandmother. The Hamlyns are apparently adamant the house stays with their family, that there is a codicil to that effect. But I am a Hamlyn, as it turns out. I was wronged, don't you see? Wronged at birth, even though it was a good deed, to save my natural mother's reputation."

So, we were Hamlyns?

"The birth certificate, though?"

My mother shrugged. "I know."

"Would they contest?"

"I'll find out more when I talk to the solicitor after Christmas, but it seems Mary looked out for me. There are documents, Tom said, that she kept in the bureau in the dining room, maybe a written statement, I don't know, but her Will is quite clear."

And that, she said, was the story of how she came to inherit a house in a village entirely owned by the Hamlyns. Because she was one. And her great-grandfather, Tristan Bray, the doctor, had left his estate to his only daughter, Mary, who'd now left it to Josie. And that was why that sly, blowsy piece, Ivy Trove, was having a go at us because of it. Jealous. Plain and simple.

"Must have hurt when she found out I'd inherited a house and land," my mother said.

"Why would she be so unpleasant about it, though?" my dad asked. "Why did she dislike you so much? Couldn't she be pleased you both had something good? Why should she want you to have nothing?"

My mum shrugged. "Some people are just like that; her daughter Beatrice is the same – got the mischief in them. She always had to be queen bee and now she's not. I'm a

Hamlyn and a landowner. She's a tenant. She was aways jealous of me, a little kid pinching my clothes and cosying up to Mum and Dad, causing trouble and friction."

I frowned. My head began to pound then, in tandem with the surf. A memory was surfacing from the back of my mind on a wave of horrible sickness.

Tamara… isn't she beautiful?

Something wasn't right, as if a jigsaw piece had been forced into a picture and made to fit. But by then they were not only holding each other's hands but squeezing them, and Mum was crying as if now totally unburdened. It was a done deal, it made sense, everyone satisfied so don't rock the boat.

"But…" I stopped. Bit my lip.

Maybe my dad hadn't noticed that photo in the Troves' sitting room? My mother's story sounded absolutely plausible, until it came to the somewhat uncomfortable and glaringly obvious fact that she looked nothing like Tamara Hamlyn. Whereas Ivy Trove was her double.

That be my mother's great-grandma, Tamara. Isn't she beautiful?"

"What is it, Enys?"

"Nothing."

But I was unsettled, a feeling that grew on returning to the house.

Dad had locked the car and Mum and I were walking up to the front door. It was dusk, the raven wings of winter had overshadowed the moors, and the house stood in darkness. A flock of crows suddenly rose from the silvery fields and trees, whirling up like scraps of charred paper from a garden fire, when the grip of her hand noticeably tensed in mine. We'd been talking about Christmas Day, about the best time to open the presents.

She saw her. I know she did. There'd been a slight movement, and we both glanced up simultaneously, just in time to see a pale face at the round window. Not an old lady staring at the lane, but a young one. A beautiful, haughty-looking one in a ruffled blouse with a beaded necklace. One who immediately reawakened my dream from the night before. Without doubt, she was identical to the lady in the photograph gracing Ivy Trove's dresser –the one my mother said was her own great-grandmother, not Ivy's.

And I swear I saw her shake her head. It wasn't over, not by a long chalk. This whole thing was going to go back so much further, so much deeper, than my mother's birth certificate and a wrangle over house deeds.

The ghosts, it seemed, were not going to lie still.

***

CHAPTER TEN

The strange thing was, after the excitement of the day I'd almost forgotten about the night to come. I think I'd made myself forget. Until we returned to the house and walked up the path.

My mother quickly recovered from what I knew she'd seen, calling over her shoulder, "We'll need some more wood bringing in, Jim!"

He already knew that, had just said as much in the car, and the words rang hollow. But she was agitated, fumbling with the front door key, telling me to leave my shoes in the hall, to hurry up and wash my hands; and the moment when I could have asked her if she'd seen the ghost at the window, was lost.

I tried so hard to think of other things, lying alone in bed that night. God knows I did – anything but wait for the click of the lock, the sound of splashing water, those terrible eyes glaring at me in the mirror. What would happen this time, now she knew I was here? Would she… I hardly dared think of it… would she speak? Would I wake to find her standing over me, consumed with rage? What could she do? What happened if you went mad?

Think of other things, Enys.

All the rivers in England, I listed them, as many as I could think of. Then all the countries around the world. Outside, the squally winds had finally dropped, replaced by an almost unearthly calm. Inside, however, the house continued to rattle, sigh and creak. I moved onto listing wild birds, telling myself all I had to do was stay awake until morning. And then she wouldn't come. While part of me, buried very deeply, part of me had wanted her to.

We'd stayed up late, playing board games. Mum and Dad downed an entire bottle of sherry, and for the first time since we'd arrived they were smiling into each other's eyes. I'd been extremely keen to keep the evening going as long as possible, to hold off the coming night, begging for another game. Just one more. It was Christmas Eve, after all. Tomorrow was Christmas and I wasn't tired enough to sleep. They wanted me to go to sleep, didn't they? One more game. Just one more and then I promise...

Eventually though, there was no avoiding the inevitable.

'Chaffinch, bullfinch, nuthatch, tree creeper, robin, fieldfare…'

The light had changed. A barn owl hooted nearby; and around the edges of the curtains, and through the gap, a starlit sky was visible, bright and clear. I tried so hard not to look, to blank out the mirror above the washstand, but there it was, I could see it out of the corner of my eye, a shining silver coin of glass.

But if you really want to know what happened in that house, because something really bad most definitely did…

'Nightingale, woodpecker, swallow…'

The slip into sleep was seamless, the jolt awake a few minutes later a shock. Immediately, I looked straight over at the washstand in the corner, heart racing, to check, to make sure. But there was no one there, and the relief then carried me away completely. It had all been a dream the night before, all a dream.

She did, however, appear that night. After my defences were down.

She came to me as she had before, in the hypnogogic state between sleep and consciousness. By degrees, I'd become aware of splashing water, telling myself there was someone in the bathroom down the hall. I would not open my eyes, I absolutely would not! I wouldn't even look.

But what happened… what happened…? Need to know…

I must have drifted away once more. When from the lower depths of sleep, an inner voice, a knowing, alerted me to the presence of someone nearby. I was floating through the murky layers where familiar figures mingle with the bizarre, before being catapulted to the surface. And into the glacial blue hush of the room. I lay panting, momentarily confused and disorientated. My breath plumed on the air like smoke.

She was here.

It took me another moment to acknowledge on some level, however, that it was not my room, not the one I'd fallen asleep in anyway, because the window behind the lady looking at me, was round. There was a periodic squeaking noise that seemed vaguely familiar, like that of a rocking cradle, and an impression of being suspended in time. The air felt charged, static. I did not have the awareness to question where I was exactly or how this could be, only that I was dreaming, albeit lucidly, and it couldn't be real. Nor was there any fear. This one didn't frighten me at all, rather I was drawn to her, the lady who sat embroidering, who when she glanced at me, it was with kindness. Dare I say, love?

"Enys! Enys, Enys…"

It was a smooth continuation of last night's dream, except whereas before she'd been content, one could say blissful, now she seemed agitated. From time to time, in a fretful manner, she glanced outside as if expecting someone imminently, scanning the lane behind before checking on me again, the smile weaker now, less reassuring. The sky, as before, was a deep, late-summer blue. But although the setting was identical, she was markedly different. Huddled into a crocheted shawl, her fingers were darting with the needle, jabbing and pulling at the embroidery with a total absence of patience, her complexion waxen and sickly, the eye sockets bruised. Was she singing, humming, mumbling? Possibly she was panting, respirations rapid and shallow, as if she couldn't catch the rhythm of her breath. Ill, I thought, desperately, appallingly ill.

Suddenly, she looked over and fixed me with the most intense, purposeful and direct stare. But the eyes were not consumed with fury and loathing like the sinister one in the mirror. Instead, they were glittering with tears, grief-stricken, the look of one who was broken, and a hand flew to her mouth in an attempt to stop herself from sobbing openly. Such a look of pleading, of desperate misery had met mine, that I was compelled to rise from the bed and go to her. But the bed, mystifyingly, was swaying and creaking, I couldn't move, and at once she threw down the embroidery ring and lunged towards me with both arms outstretched.

Which was when I registered the strange pinpoint pupils, and that her hands were all scratched and bleeding, her white cotton blouse smeared strawberry red. The same? Was this also the woman who'd been at the wash basin?

The scary one? Because the two appeared to merge…

A blood curdling scream then ejected me out of the dream. Was that me? Had I screamed?

Someone was running down the corridor.

To my horror, however, the footsteps continued past the door. Not towards me at all, but straight past.

***

Chapter Eleven

The confusion was immense. I sat up, had no idea where I was. Then gradually it filtered back in – this was the house in Devon – there was the washstand in the corner, the wardrobe filled with fur stoles and flowery dresses, and I'd dreamt of the woman at the window again.

But who had screamed? Because someone had definitely run past the door, their footsteps quick and light. I could not make sense of it. If that was my mother, then surely she'd have come to me, to this room?

Who then?

Willing the bathroom door to click, the toilet to flush, for a rational explanation, I sat shivering, staring at the shadowy outline of the door. Whoever it was hadn't put a light on, not even a lamp in their room. Nor were there any comforting sounds of normality. Instead, crawling over me was the most uncomfortable feeling, some vague dread… followed by a draught, only a slight one, but a waft of cooler air around my face as if the door, which had been left slightly ajar, had just opened further.

I heard it then, for the second time, and the breath caught in my throat, lodging like a small, hard stone. This was all real. Had not been my imagination. A delicate rustle, like that of a silken gown, or the wing of a bird. Breathe and you'd miss it. Someone was just outside the door!

In the soft, dove-grey light the threshold was silent and still: no shadows flitted, no movement to trick the eye. I stared and stared until my eyes burned, could not afford to blink – someone was there for sure. I could hear them breathing.

Enys… Enys…

Again came a waft of cold air, but this time it seemed to emanate from the corridor, and immediately I remembered the person running past. Not an old lady tap-tap-tapping with a stick, but the solid footsteps of a real person. One of my parents had left a door open! That would be it. Relief washed over me, at the same time as worry that something was badly amiss. And so, cautiously, I swung my legs over the side of the small iron bed frame, padded barefoot towards the door, and stepped onto the shadowy landing. Shivering uncontrollably, teeth chattering, I made my way tentatively along the creaking corridor towards my parents' room. The midnight air was icy but, as my eyes became accustomed to the gloom, I could see a door open ahead. Pearlescent moonlight bathed the corridor, and it was then I saw, with a stab of shock, that the open door belonged to the middle bedroom, the one with the round window – the one we'd locked.

Enys… Enys…

Not my parents' room. Had I imagined the footsteps, too? Had it been a trick? A figment of a dream? Nevertheless, I kept on walking, the pull magnetic.

Enys… Enys…

I had to know, just had to look, to see… Would she be there?

On reaching the doorway, I stopped, and slowly turned,

knowing, expecting, to see her at the window, for her to beckon to me. This was the blurring of a dream, not real, not real… And it was never in question that I wouldn't go to her. Not only would I go, I would do whatever she wanted, I knew I would.

And so what I saw took a while to comprehend: the difference between the dreamlike expectation and the reality.

The woman in the pale nightdress was sitting exactly where she'd been in the dream, on the window seat. There were no curtains in that room, and she was clearly silhouetted, by the bluish-whiteness of snow-reflected light. Behind her, white flakes were fluttering out of the night sky like goose down, the moors behind a breath-taking white-out.

Snowing! Narnia….

I struggled to make sense of it: on one level, here was a woman in exactly the same position as the one in my dream, I had heard the rustle of her dress, heard her call my name; yet on the other, the room was cluttered with upended furniture and boxes, and it was snowing.

My mother was looking straight through me, as if she had no clue who I was, her eyes glazed and unseeing, hair a dark nest of disarray. For a few moments we both stared at each other, shivering and confused. She wasn't moving at all, or speaking. As soon as I realised it was her, alarm quickly spread through me and I hurried over. She was cold like death, like night, her arm marble to the touch. I was frightened, wondering what was wrong with her.

"Mum, you need to go back to bed."

Without a word or any resistance, she allowed herself to be led back to her bedroom, a wraith gliding beside me, ethereal and dreamy. Dad turned over and muttered as I pushed her onto the bed, but she lay gently down of her own accord, and I pulled the blankets over her as if she'd been a sleepwalking child and I the mother.

At least I knew who'd run down the corridor, and I was satisfied with that, conveniently ignoring nagging inconsistencies, as I hurried back to bed and jumped in. There was snow out there, it was Christmas, a white Christmas, and dawn was almost here. Now I could sleep. It was my mother who'd been opening the door at night, and she who'd caused the draught and shadowed the doorway; the apparition in the mirror was a bad dream and nothing more. How convincing the mind can be! Even when little knots begin to form in the gut and the details don't fit at all. But that's what I persuaded myself was true, at least for a while, and looking back it's probably just as well or I'd never have slept at all.

Next day my mother had shadowed eye sockets and her skin was ashen.

"Think I'm coming down with a bug, Jim," she said, loading the turkey into the range. "I can't stop shivering and I haven't slept a wink."

She did look awful, and I repeatedly caught her watching me. Why, though? She couldn't remember sleepwalking, she said, even denying it as possible. But why would she think I'd make that up? I began to doubt the whole thing, to mistrust my own memory then. In fact, there was a surreal feeling to the whole day, an unsettled one from start to finish. And my, what a finish! But we were yet to find that out.

Snow lit the view in a glare of white from every window, a fall that had put down several inches overnight, transforming the scene into an Alpine landscape. When I went to fill the wood baskets, my footsteps pressed and creaked, the prints a single trail in the unsullied surface from the back door to the barn. The cold was stinging, it chapped the face and nipped the ears, gusts of wind whipping up sparkling crystals that swept across the fields. And towering over the valley, the stone circle stood atop the hill like petrified druids, solid and eternal, the austere landscape unchanging, a powerful reminder of our transience. I stopped mid-task, mesmerised by the frozen beauty. Narnia, I thought, we were in Narnia.

It was, however, to be the oddest day of my life, of all our lives.

It started off strangely and continued that way, an incremental build-up, a series of omens, although we didn't recognise them as such. Everything was put down to coincidence, this or that, all explainable if you didn't see the whole. We hadn't been able to get a fire going – not at all, in any room, using any method. Although well-seasoned, the wood would not catch, smoking profusely instead, a damp squib. In the absence of any other form of heating, the house was bone-chilling. Some of the pipes were frozen, a picture fell off the wall, and then a bulb blew and the electrics fused. One calamity occurred after another and as fast as they were fixed, another one happened. We did, however, eventually sit down to Christmas Dinner, even though the festive candles bought at the market flickered out and the room was hazy with smoke.

My present had been a soft toy, a dog with silky golden fur and a red ribbon collar with a bell, the only one I remember. Perhaps it was the last childish thing I had? It was also the last year I got a pound note from 'Aunty Ivy,

Uncle George and Cousin Beatrice'. It came with a carton of Quality Street chocolates and a surprise that had me squealing with delight, a pair of white, lacy tights just like Beatrice's.

"You'll have to go and thank her," my mother said, unwrapping her own present from Ivy. She'd kept it until last. "Wonder what it'll be this year? Let me guess!"

Her face was a picture. We'd been invited for Christmas Dinner at the farm, but I'm guessing Mum, perhaps wisely, made some excuse. It was, anyway, Round Four to my mother.

She unwrapped the same bottle of lily of the valley she'd given to Ivy last year from the shop, and now, it seemed, she had it back.

"Still got the label on as well," she said, then smiled. "Mind you, you ought to see what I sent her."

"What?"

"A pinny with a diet sheet on the front. 'How to lose weight in ten days.'"

"But she's not fat."

"She'm a great heffer, Enys," my mother snapped. "And so would I be if I ate as many cakes as her. Anyway, imagine her face when she opens that!"

Dad had laughed, a great, roaring guffaw that sounded more like a pressure valve being released than genuine humour, but it was needed and we laughed, the mood lifted. And we carried on giggling as we pulled the crackers bought at the market. Each, of course, contained a paper hat, a silly toy, and a joke to read aloud. Mine and Dad's were totally unmemorable. But Mum's wasn't. And the laughter died on her face in an instant.

How it could have happened, who knows? But her

message, and she'd already blurted it out, had been, 'You won't be laughing soon.'

Ghosts don't lie still...

All the remaining colour drained from her face, she knocked over a glass and rushed from the room. Some kind of sick joke, she said later, and whoever could have done it? We didn't know. Dad suggested that as we'd bought them from the market, we didn't know where they'd come from, that there were all sorts of people out there, mad as snakes, mean-spirited. It was just coincidence and shouldn't spoil our day.

Perhaps, however, we should have thanked the series of unnerving things that happened that day, because they psychologically paved the way for what was to come. We were already spooked, on edge, Dad drinking a tad too much, my mother restless, jumping up and down to tend the fire, or fetch more of this, that or the other from the kitchen. But it was, looking back, as if we all knew to expect something else. We just didn't know what. Or, in my case, when.

But just as we finished the meal, at six o'clock precisely there came a thundering knock at the door.

... That be on Christmas Day about six o'clock, so I expect he might come to you afore then...

My heart leapt like a cuckoo out of a clock. And my mother's glance instantly shot to me. *You knew!*

But by then it was too late.

I'd be glad if you told me dreckly, what the real story is, because he's the only one who'll know... So, make sure to ask him, won't you? When he says story or song? Say 'Story!'

***

PART TWO
The Droll Teller

'Only the dose makes the poison.'
Paracelsus

CHAPTER TWELVE

Gorse Bank House, Christmas Day

Silas Finn stood in the entrance porch, a grizzled, weather-beaten figure holding a lantern in one hand and a fiddle in the other. Behind him, beneath a starlit sky, snow had weighed down the arms of the firs and piled on the barn roofs, the whiteness stark, frosty and icily glittering.

"Good evening, sir, madam. Season's greetings and a very merry Christmas to you. Silas Finn at your service."

"And to you, sir," said James Quiller.

"'Tis a long while since this grand house be inhabited by a family," said Silas, nodding at the child half hiding behind her father. "And even longer since I last had occasion to visit." He lifted his hat and made a small, old-fashioned bow before addressing Josie. "But as ee knows, madam, 'tis tradition a droll teller come to a new owner, to offer a story or a song."

"Come inside, man. It's freezing out there," said James. "Would you like a glass of sherry? We'd love a song, I think, wouldn't we, Enys?"

The man stamped snow off his boots. "Ah, Enys, is it?

That be a beautiful name. Beautiful. Takes me back a long way, that does!"

"Well, we mustn't keep you too long, Mr Finn. You'll be on your way to Trewhella Farm dreckly after this, I expect? For the barn dance?"

His brown eyes sparkled beneath bushy brows dusted with snow – brows that sprang around in corkscrews of white and silver. He wore a harum-scarum overcoat, work boots, and a hand-knitted scarf wound around his neck. From under a battered trilby, curly grey hair leapt out in damp tendrils, his complexion ruddy and as deeply lined as a walnut.

James ushered him inside. "Come and have a warm. Just you, is it?"

"Aye, sir. The other scrapers be at the farm. I'll catch 'em later, I'm in no hurry, sir."

James shut the porch door and Silas blew into the hall.

"Come through. I'm afraid we've had the devil's own getting the fire going today, but it's crackling away now. I'm James Quiller by the way, and this is my wife, Josie."

Once by the fire, he handed the stranger a glass of sherry, which Silas, after warming his hands over the flames for a moment, thanked him for and then set it down on the mantelpiece.

"We can offer tea instead? How about a mince pie? Bought not made this year, I'm afraid, but from the market in Gulston, pretty good actually."

"Thank ee, sir. Thank ee kindly, but I won't partake until I've entertained ee, as is the custom." Addressing Josie directly, he added, "As you'll know, as you'll remember, madam."

Josie frowned slightly.

"This old place hasn't changed a bit," he said, looking round at the walls flickering with shadows, display cabinets and paintings. "Strange thing, time. It must be decades, yet it seems only yesterday I stood in this exact same spot. There's even the old bureau there by the window, just like it was last time. Same place."

"Really? How–"

"Well, what tune shall we have?" Josie said. "Sorry, Jimmy. I didn't mean to butt in. What would you like to play for us, Mr Finn? We mustn't hold you up – I'm sure you'll be wanting to join the others and there's only the three of us here."

Silas nodded and put the fiddle to his chin. "There be no rush, madam. Not from me, no, never was I one to rush, but I may suggest this–"

"No!" Enys said. "No, a story. Please will you tell us a story instead?"

James laughed. "Enys! Let the man play–"

"No, I want a story."

"Enys, stop it. The gentleman's got a long walk down to the farm and he hasn't got time to–"

"Oh, that's all right, madam. The farm be nearby and the night not so cruel cold for one such as me. There be plenty of time to tell ee a story, 'tis my pleasure, although a tune before we begin wouldn't go amiss."

"All right, well what about telling Enys the one about giants on Bodmin Moor and how the standing stones got there? Or the mermaid and the doom bar? Yes, that would be a good one."

"Or the hounds of Dartmoor?" James added. "A Conan Doyle story?"

Silas narrowed his eyes, considering, and then after a

moment, nodded and took the seat by the fire James was encouraging him to take, keeping the fiddle poised to his chin.

"We're grateful for whichever you prefer," James was saying. "It's all new to Enys and I, we're fascinated by all the old stories. And Enys loves fairy tales."

"From the village, are you, madam?" Silas asked, settling into the armchair. "Only I have this feeling I seen you afore."

"Goodness, what a memory. I'm afraid I don't remember much. I left when I was little more than a child."

He nodded again. And then the lights in his eyes fired bright as embers. "I know, I'll play a partic'l'r tune while I think what story to tell ee. There's one I'm thinking of that might interest ee. You may have heard it told afore, madam, or you may not have." He pulled back the bow to play.

"Are you very old?" Enys asked, just as the first note sounded.

He tilted back his head and laughed, revealing a higgledy-piggledy collection of tombstone teeth.

"Did you know my great-grandmother, Mary? Only she used to live here."

"I wouldn't say I knew the lady but I met her once, when I came to visit soon after she took over the house." Again he addressed Josie. "As you surely know, all new owners be paid a visit? But this story be from long afore Mary's time. And who's to say if it carries truth or if it don't? 'Tis just a story, see? Just a story."

"Well, what a coincidence." said James. "Mary left this house to my wife, Mr Finn. We found out less than a week ago. We're the new owners but are only here for a few days.

What timing!"

Silas put a hand to his heart. "God rest her soul. May her spirit be at peace now, sir."

He settled the violin beneath his chin once more and pulled back the bow. A strangely haunting melody then ensued, deep and resonant, music that felt both ancient and yet familiar to the listener, as if they'd known it all their lives, one that felt to each as if it took them home. Vibrating within the chambers of the heart, it stirred up deep wells of long-dormant emotions, tugging and loosening the strings of the soul, prising it from all matters earthly. So, too, it drew out hovering shadows from the corners of the room and caused the fire to flare and burn more intensely; the old man's eyes glinting starlit pools as the melody lulled and calmed all those present. The atmosphere shifted, it seemed, to another realm, another time and place, silencing questions that had formed, quelling all further thoughts, taking those present on a journey to a faraway place, one of only their own knowing. They became wholly entranced, rendered inert and helpless for the duration, mesmerised by the leaping, flickering flames of the fire, the rest of the room a black cave of nothingness.

Enys had sunk onto the hearthrug. James relaxed against the back of the sofa and Josie had long since put down her glass of sherry.

And even after the final notes had trailed away, the vibration continued, its magic replaying behind the shades of the eyes, continuing to echo through minds that danced with unseen images, unspoken poetry, and swirling emotions.

Breaking the silence that followed, punctuated only by

the hiss of the fire, the occasional crack and splintering of a log, Enys asked, "Do you remember Victorian times, Mr Finn?"

"Why, yes," Silas replied. "I remember everything, child. That's why I goes about telling these stories, see? So's they won't get lost along the way. Lest anyone forgets." He rested the violin against the inglenook. "And this one I'm going to tell ee be a good one. A mighty good one. Coming to me nice and clear now, it is!"

Enys suddenly winged around as sharply as if she'd been stung on the back of the neck, at the same time as Josie.

Both turned back simultaneously.

Enys shrugged. "Sorry, I thought the door opened."

"It's just a draught. Place is full of them. Do go on, Mr Finn," said James, his voice distant and disconnected, barely heard by the others, a spectator from the stalls of a theatre.

And then the tale was finally told. One that could no longer be stopped. For no one quite knew what he was going to say, least of all the droll teller himself.

***

CHAPTER THIRTEEN

"There's an old wind-blasted inn perched up on the headland, about halfway between The Lizard and Land's End. Wheeler Jack's, they call it. You know the kind of place, Mr Quiller, where–?"

"James. Please, call me James."

Silas nodded. "James. Been there centuries has that inn, James. Cob walls several feet deep and by God you need 'em when a storm's blowing up. One of those hidden places you wouldn't know was there, like an abandoned old kiddleywink, tucked over the brow of the cliffs. There's a steep set of steps down one side and a thick oak door with a No Entry sign..." He laughed. "But go in, dip your head under the beam, and you'll find a hotchpotch of dark timber rooms. Never changes - tobacco and lamp oil ingrained in the woodwork, same grizzly old seadogs staring out to sea. They'll not look up when you walk in neither, seeing as how no stranger will ever find his way there.

"Ah, but you could sit and look at that bay all day long, watching the light change on the water. Some days that ocean be gunmetal grey and so angry it'll hit the window hard enough to shatter it. And then there be those magical times, at sunset, when it stretches out in a film of liquid gold, the sky all ablaze. But you'll never tire of it...Never tire..."

He smiled. "Well, the light was beginning to fade that summer evening when my friend and I walked in. The incoming tide was washing on the rocks below, there was the clink of glasses, and murmur of conversation in the booths – bit louder than usual that evening though, and a few raised voices. It was getting late, and the drink had been flowing a fair few hours.

"We'd had a good day if I remember rightly, myself and my good companion, crowding in the town square, made a few shillings apiece." He glanced over at the hat he'd placed on the mantelpiece. "Seen a few public houses in its time, has that hat. And the inside of a few hundred barns and stables, too, including this one."

James nodded, prompting him to continue, for the man was good at what he did, his voice lilting, melodic.

"But on this partic'l'r night the talk was somewhat different and we both of us picked that up right away, soon as we walked in. The atmosphere was charged, see? A few sparks were flying. Transpired one of our fellow crowders was in that evening; he'd been travelling up this way, weaving across country, and had almost reached Fowey when a piece of shocking news caught up with him. News that concerns this village you now reside in, Hunters Combe.

"The fella's name was Connor, a friend I've travelled with many times, and it turned out he was one of the last folks to see her alive. She was dead, see, all of a sudden? Tamara Hamlyn. She'd be Mary's mother, your great-grandmother, Mrs Quiller? Thing was, though, she was cruel young, and although she'd been pale, which would be natural enough in her condition, she'd been especially vigorous, he said, when he'd seen her last. Vigorous to the point of her being agitated, and he'd seen her alive not a few days afore. It didn't feel right in his bones, he said, that she'd died so sudden like that, especially when there'd been such a scandal the very same day. A scandal as big as they come. And the more he thought about the matter, the more it hadn't sat well with him, although he couldn't say for sure, as to exactly why that might be.

"Now, the talk here in the village had been about her and a young chap, that they'd been carrying on extra-maritally, you might say? A course, I don't know anything about the matter but it's how it started and the story grew. She'd been seen with Jowen Trewhella, a foreman and engineer at the mine just beyond Hounds Tor. You'd have passed the old pit chimney if you came in on that road from up along? Closed down now a course, closed a long time since, but back then he'd be one of those involved in the closures, and the new rail tracks built at Withyarm Marsh. Supposed to have been doing very well for himself by all accounts, one of the Trewhella farming lads, but very ambitious, very bright, got in with certain types that could elevate your status in life, if you get my drift?"

James leaned forward, nodding.

"Well, as I'm sure ee can imagine, when the knowledge about the pair got out it be like a fox in a chicken coop, especially with 'er being a Hamlyn and her father the local parson. The talk was everywhere in the village and beginning to spread further afield–"

Enys started to ask, "What's extra-mari–"

"It doesn't matter, Enys. Just means they liked each other and the lady was married. It wasn't done for women to have male friends. Actually, it's way past your bedtime, come to think of it."

"What? Oh no, please! That's not fair, it's not even seven o'clock yet. I can't!"

"I know, but it's been a long day and this is most definitely a story for adults."

"No, I've got to hear it. You don't understand."

James shook his head. "Do as your mother says, Enys. Go and get ready for bed. No arguments."

Josie stood up. "Do you mind waiting a few minutes, Mr Finn?"

"I don't rush, Mrs Quiller. You take your time."

But Josie did rush. While the two men chatted amiably enough about the weather and the roads being blocked with snow, she quickly made Ovaltine and sorted out a hot water bottle for Enys, who'd stomped furiously upstairs. And when she returned a matter of minutes later, James was putting another log on the fire and refilling the sherry glasses.

"Sorry about that, but if this is going to be about an affair or a crime of passion, it's probably best. She's ever so cross, but she's far too young for that kind of thing."

Silas nodded. "I have no doubt you're right, no doubt at all."

"Do go on," said James. "I'd really like to hear."

"So would I."

Silas smiled kindly, and the story was continued.

"It be a lonely game at times, wandering the lanes for days and days, sometimes without a companion, other times with. But there be many an hour to mull things over. And so when our friend, Connor, heard Tamara was dead it struck a wrong chord. Last time he'd seen her she'd been excitable, see? Almost in a frenzy, unable to stand still, she'd constantly glanced up the lane, every few seconds he said, as if expecting someone. He'd been walking down from Hounds Tor towards the village when she'd rushed out of the house and waylaid him, a most surprising and unusual behaviour in itself, her never having taken much notice of him afore. And the day he was certain of, including the time, it being just afore the guldize – that's a feast of the hayricks, sir. I'm sure Mrs Quiller knows about those, but that partic'l'r year, Connor be the fiddler on his way to Trewhella Farm, as is tradition, and very generous the Trewhellas always were, too. But that was when ee seen her last, Tamara Hamlyn, and that be what he remembered. There be more about that encounter, and I'll come back to it in a moment.

"Thing was, that same evening at the guldize, and this be what set him thinking when he heard the news – instead of the usual jollity there'd been a terrible set-to. As it turned out, certain folks were upset for different reasons, but the more ale and cider they sank, the more tongues had loosened. And after a while, mutterings under the breath erupted into taunts, accusations and outright jibes with some spoiling for a fight.

"Jowen Trewhella was there, although not, a course, Tamara. However, the doctor, Tristan Bray, the lady's husband, was.

"A course, I don't have a record of what was said that evening, other than hearsay from an honest friend, who had nothing to gain in the telling. But there's no doubting after that night it blew up into a mighty scandal, with folks talking about it openly on front doorsteps far and wide, well beyond Hunters Combe. And some would say it all be gossip and that may be, except the lady died a few days later, and then there was a terrible accident."

He paused a moment, looking into the far recess of the fire.

A log cracked and spat.

"I was little more than a nipper that night at Wheeler Jack's – maybe ten, maybe twelve – that's how it was and no one asked. You've to remember they were very different times and not so bad for that. I was free as a lark, spent many a day lying in a meadow or a sand dune gazing up at the sky, had just what I needed, no more, no less… wouldn't change it…"

"Not even on a night like this?" Josie asked.

"Not even on a night like this, Mrs Quiller. There be a nice warm barn at Trewhella tonight, good company, food, music, and stories. Depends how you want to look at the life journey, 'cause there be many different ways. Thing is, I never forget a thing, and now it's all flowing back to me, like an incoming tide."

He shook his head.

"Many layers though, so many layers to this one… But words were spoken that evening at the guldize that could not be taken back. And afterwards, those words travelled. All the way to Tamara's father at the vicarage, Lord and Lady Hamlyn at the big house, and to everyone in between.

"It was strongly speculated, see, that Tamara Hamlyn's first child was not her husband's, but in fact Jowen Trewhella's; that the child resembled him more and more with each passing day and it was impossible to deny. The lad, Christopher, did look just like him, it had to be said. And now it was openly discussed, folks were saying how could they not have seen it afore? Christopher had the same wide-spaced, steady brown eyes as Jowen. Nothing like Doctor Bray, whose pale eyes were remarkably close together, his face long, the chin pointed. Oh, the boy had his mother's fine bones, but it was the eyes that spoke the truth of the matter: look at the child and you saw Jowen Trewhella's mirror image. He had the same sturdiness to him as well, stocky and strong. And now she had another on the way!

"The pair had been seen, too, walking in the woods by the river when the good doctor was away, and up at the stone circle, as you can see from the windows here. There was a derelict cottage up there, an old miner's place, and it was said they met there.

"Well, the gossip ignited at the guldize – how all of a sudden it made sense she'd sit in that window all day, which wasn't decent, not decent at all. It would be so she could wave to Jowen Trewhella as he rode home from Withyarm Marsh of an evening, past the Tailor's Rest and down the lane to the village. How she'd always be there and they'd all seen her, could all attest to it. Some said of course she'd be there, it was the nursery, and others said no, she had a maid, and wouldn't the lady of the house do her needlepoint in the sitting room overlooking the lawns? Especially one brought up at the vicarage, her father a Hamlyn? How brazen, how outrageous, to be waiting on another fellow in that condition!

"Seemed the free flow of drink had released the genie from the bottle, and what had been idle speculation up until then, became true. So there Trewhella and Bray were, sitting opposite each other, being goaded. How Tamara was no better than she ought to be, and what was the doctor going to do about it, and how if it was their wife, then Jowen Trewhella would be laid out flat by now.

"Jowen was openly challenged to deny it, not by Bray,

but what could he do? As a God-loving man, we can presume he'd not wished to lie or deny his own son. Maybe the pair had planned to run away together? The Hamlyns would never have consented to their union, and certainly not after she'd married and borne a child, with another on the way. But if he confessed, what would happen to her? These were very different times. She could be cast out."

"He was a fool," said James.

"And a cheat," said Josie.

"Aye, and he was judged and found wanting, that be so – a lovesick fool, they all said it," Silas agreed. "But then again, you should have seen her!"

There was a pause, a slight stiffening, and a small, surprised start of alarm glimpsed in the depth of Josie Quiller's eyes.

"My God, but he was only flesh and blood and I ain't never seen a woman like her neither afore nor since. Ivy Trove's a pale imitation, and that's saying something, eh? There's probably only me now to vouch for it; but just like Ivy, Tamara Hamlyn had the same bit of flirtatiousness about her too, a spark in the eye that made a man's pulse quicken, a reputation that no doubt made the situation a whole lot worse for her. She'd no close women friends, see? No one to give her level-headed advice, to confide in. Opposite, in fact. Seems the womenfolk round here put the boot in, even her own family. And days later, this perfec'ly healthy woman was stone dead. Yet according to my good friend she'd looked perfec'ly well and not due for a good couple of months. Told him as much.

"But maybe it would have ended there, all the same. Many women died in childbirth, even those with comfortable lives and doctors for husbands, and p'r'aps she was unduly stressed by the gossip?"

Josie nodded.

"But then time, as time is wont to do, began to unravel a few inconsistencies with the accepted story, you might say. Now it could be we travellers, not being embroiled in the daily turmoil of life, may see matters more clearly? That we hear many a different perspective? Or maybe we be on our own too long? But the question the old boys were wrangling over at Wheeler Jack's that evening was this: 'had there been foul play?'

"It wasn't as simple as was made out, see? The explanation was a bit too convenient, too lazy. There were a lot of folks whose problems would be solved with her death. And the more information as came out later, the more it didn't sit right. But I'll have to tell ee about Tamara first. If you recall, I said I'd come back to when Connor met her in the lane?"

***

CHAPTER FOURTEEN

"That time I seen Tamara Hamlyn would've been the first summer my uncle Gil took me on the road with him, and seeing as I was one of eight in a two-bed cottage, I gladly went. Never went back home again, neither. 'Twas he who taught me the fiddle like it's a second skin. I'd tag along with him from town to town, farm to farm, learning everything I could, listening to stories all the way from Land's End to Hounds Tor.

"I been doing that for a long, long time and you'd think all those memories'd be a blur, but I remember that day clear as a spring water well, standing in this very room and gawping at her like she be the Queen of Sheba. It would've been the tail end of summer, working our way over from Gulston to Fowey, and I couldn't tell you what songs were played or who else was in the room, but I do remember her.

"See, there was an unworldly element about her, a golden light within, not like other people. Quite haughty-looking she was, with a high-bridged nose, straight brow, and eyes that were emerald, the brightest, deepest green you've ever seen. Mermaid green, they'd say down Helston way. Thing was, it didn't matter which way she turned, this way or that, it was the kind of beauty that entranced, a work of art that caught in candlelight like a cut diamond, and I couldn't take my eyes off her. Must have been about nine or ten years old, I expect. But I never knew my birth date or counted the years, so like I said, the night I heard the news at Wheeler Jack's I'd probably been about twelve. Like a knife to the stomach, it was. Shook me up quite bad!

"See 'ere, so I'll tell ee now about the day Connor met her on the lane. You remember how folks said her lad, Christopher, looked the image of Jowen Trewhella? Well, that day he saw the child for himself. He'd been on his way down to the village when he looked up and saw them both at the round window, staring out just like everyone said. She paused her needlepoint, watched until he drew level, then to his amazement, waved for him to stop. He'd been heading to Trewhella Farm for the guldize, and it seemed she wanted to know who else would be there that evening. Told him she wished to go, but her husband said it would not be wise in her condition, and with him being a doctor she felt she must listen, but oh, how she'd wanted to.

"But the most marked thing about her was the extreme, in his words, agitation that had completely taken hold of her. Gone was the golden essence of the woman, the flashing green eyes, the calm, light-hearted demeanour. Pacing back and forth, she was dreadful white, he said, constantly glancing up the lane as I told ee. But the impression he had was that ee wasn't partic'l'r interested in him, instead deliberately delaying him, that the talk was somewhat strained as she asked about every last member of his acquaintance. Eventually, a course, she could stretch it out no longer.

"At the time, not thinking too hard about the matter, he put the lady's whey-faced complexion down to her condition, that she'd be indoors more than usual, and didn't consider it untoward until much later, when there were many miles of distance between them. She'd been more than pale, he reflected, far more. Her skin had an unnatural, almost translucent white sheen. And her eyes had changed. Again, it didn't strike him until days later, quite what had disturbed him, but the last time he'd seen her, and most definitely when I had, her eyes were spellbinding, sparkling the way the sun glints on water. But on that day, he said you wouldn't have even noticed the colour, only the tiny, mad-looking pinpoint pupils. And it fair set him at odds with himself."

Josie put a hand to her throat.

"There was one other thing, too – she'd been wearing gloves. And she certainly hadn't been wearing them when sewing at the window a few moments afore.

"None of this registered with him, mind, 'til it churned over and over in his mind and occurred to him as strange. How she'd waved to him frantically to wait, had gone to the trouble to put gloves on, then waylaid him so long he hadn't known what else to say, only that he needed to go, that the others be waiting for him in the barn."

Silas paused a few moments before continuing.

"In short, she'd been in a fervour that was not in keeping with her character – a woman of such self-possession as to be mischievous, the type as could work a room into a bee-frenzy, then step back and calmly admire the handywork. Yet there she'd been, all worked up herself. But not fatigued, my friend said, not ill, definitely not at death's door."

"Laudanum?" James asked. "Just thinking about the complexion and constricted pupils. Could be the same reason for covering her hands, too – if they were itchy, that she'd scratched them. I'm just wondering if she died from laudanum poisoning?"

"Could be, sir. Was a popular medication at the time. On prescription only by then, a course, but aye, 't would be used common enough and she'd have access to it with her husband being the doctor. Mrs Winslow's Soothing Syrup, you'll recall? Used by nursemaids for kiddies, too."

"Godfrey's Cordial."

"Yes, and as you say it might've explained the lady's demise. Save for one thing."

"Oh?"

"Pardon me but I'll come back to that if ee don't mind, Mr Quiller, because there's her husband, Doctor Bray, I've to tell ee about. Now, I didn't recall him to look at, never noticed him 'til his photograph appeared in the newspapers and my memory was jolted. Dour-looking fellow, kind of lurked like a shadow, tall and spiky-boned, all fingers, elbows and knees. Pointy beard and moustache. The eyes, though, awful close together they were, pale as glass. Not unpopular, I have to say, not at all – a busy country doctor – folks liked him, respected him. He saw to the sick, the dying, colicky children. He and his nurse, Nancy, turned out in all weathers, day or night, nothing too much trouble. Not only that but he'd take payment from those who couldn't afford the fee, with, say, a chicken or a few logs, often giving medicine without charge."

"Decent chap?"

"Indeed. But there hung what you might call an imbalance, see? Tamara not only had the beauty, but the money, too – serious money – and it was she who'd been given thc house. In other words, she owned everything and he nothing. Her father had the vicarage, but with two older sisters as yet unmarried and her the way she was, they married her off to the local doctor before you could say Jack Sprat. Wed afore she was out of her teens.

"Thing was, it seems Tamara wasn't quite as pleased with the arrangement as everyone else, because afore long there be rumours of her and young Jowen. And in contrast to Bray, Jowen was an exceptionally good-looking lad. Not only that, but he'd attracted a fair few county women and local maids alike. So, there be more than a bit of bad feeling stirred up when it turned out he'd got the glad eye for Tamara Hamlyn. No one was happy about what they heard, not her family, not the local women, not her husband; and so the simmering pot began to boil and spit until it finally spilled over that night at the guldize. And Doctor Bray could ignore it no longer.

"She wasn't there, a course. We can only imagine her stuck inside the house, pacing up and down, staring out the window on the top floor, wondering what was being said about her. Maybe hoping Jowen would come for her and Christopher? We can't know, and p'r'aps we'll never know.

"But one thing we can say is that after that night, no one ever saw her alive again, not outside this house, anyway.

"But remember I told you there were inconsistencies and events further down the line that called into question the accepted story, one of the many reasons there were raised voices in Wheeler Jack's that night? Well, this was the first and it wasn't long after. In church the following week, Tristan Bray spoke at his wife's funeral, and according to the housekeeper, Duffy Piper, who I'll tell ee more about shortly, Bray stood in the pulpit and informed the church congregation that Tamara had died in childbirth after suffering for months from myeloid leukaemia.

"Dreadful shocked was Duffy Piper, it being the first she knew of it. And barely did she hear the rest of what he said, but he'd gone on to explain Tamara hadn't wanted anyone to know for fear of upsetting those she loved. Both sisters were present in the family pew, both in tears. Tamara had hoped, he said, to see the pregnancy to full term but the fatigue had been too great. Luckily, however, the child had survived, a near miracle, which was testimony only to the expertise and skill of his nurse, local midwife Nancy Peller.

"And so grateful was he to Nancy Peller, that only a few months later he married her."

Josie gasped. "He married the nurse?"

Silas nodded. "Oh yes, little flaxen-haired Nancy. Married her, some said, in unseemly haste."

***

CHAPTER FIFTEEN

"When Tristan married Nancy Peller, most folks cheered. Who could blame him, they said, after the way Tamara behaved – flaunting an affair in front of his face, the good doctor now left with a baby to bring up, not to mention another man's child? Others, though… well, they said how terrible it was she'd been taken so ill, and what a burden to have had to keep it to herself –God alone knows what she must have suffered and it be awful sad. The pendulum swung a little with that wedding, see, a few folks no doubt feeling a twinge of guilt for their part in spiteful talk now the lady was dead.

"But everyone was glad the child had survived, that some good had come of it all, and despite malicious speculation to the contrary, the little girl looked nothing like Jowen Trewhella, or even Tamara. In fact, Mary Rose be a dead ringer for her father, Tristan Bray, and there was relief in that. Aye, there be relief in that…"

James and Josie agreed.

"In short, the tragedy of her death had been explained, and in deference to the Hamlyn family, all further gossip should now cease. It had been upsetting enough."

"Absolutely," said Josie.

"Alas, a few inconvenient truths began to surface."

He paused for a moment before continuing.

"See, there were staff in the house – remember the housekeeper, Duffy Piper? She and her husband, Jan, had a set of rooms on the ground floor here."

"Ah! I wondered what they were for," James said. "Should have guessed. We closed those off, they're freezing."

"I imagine they would be, Mr Quiller, with the fires not kept in. I knew them both personal though, and can vouch for this part of the story myself. See, Jan frequented The Tailor's Rest up the lane 'ere, and Duffy we'd see in Gulston market. But it was Mrs Piper who walked out of the funeral that day. Stood up alone, she did, footsteps echoing as she walked back down the aisle, Tristan Bray's eyes burning into her back. Said her hands were shaking and she didn't know what to do with herself, except she couldn't sit for another second and listen to what she knew was lies, especially not in a House of God.

"But even then she'd not spoken out. Not in the village. Not officially. See, these rooms may seem drear to you, but to Duffy and Jan, especially at their time of life, that be a roof over their heads, Mr Quiller. That be a roof!"

"Yes." James nodded. "Yes, of course. I see."

"But just like Connor, Duffy Piper had felt things queer from the start. She could speak to me and Gil, see, we crowders being, as you might say, of no consequence to anyone, nothing to lose, our word not counting for much. And so we sat on the quayside one day, years later mind, at Gulston. And she told us that when Dr Bray stood in the pulpit and told everyone Tamara had been extremely fatigued due to leukaemia, that she'd hung on valiantly for as long as she could for the sake of the unborn child, she'd rushed out, in her own words, 'beside herself.' Nor had she gone to the vicarage afterwards for brandy and refreshments, even though as housekeeper she'd been invited. Her husband had, mind. Jan went. Indeed, he'd partaken to excess of all available spirits. But he'd uttered not one word, either to her or anyone else, about what the doctor had said that day. Not a peep. And so she'd been alone with what she knew. Alone until the bitter end when her very sanity was at stake. But we'll come back to the Pipers in a moment. Because long before Duffy Piper spoke a word about anything, there was a terrible and most unfortunate accident.

"It happened up at the new railway line. They'd been collapsing a tunnel when some heavy machinery had fallen, trapping Jowen Trewhella's leg. Dr Bray was away in another village so they sent for Jowen's father, Joss. He managed to get the lad back to the farm by pony and trap, where his family bathed him and put him to bed. You might think the Trewhellas would have disowned Jowen after the scandal with Tamara, but far from it – they closed around him, protected him, said he'd suffered enough.

"I knew Joss Trewhella pretty well as a matter of fact, but it was to be many a year before he spoke about what happened to Jowen. That would've been in The Tailor's Rest one evening. Took it bad, he did, really bad, was never the same again and rarely spoke of it to anyone.

"The lad, he said, had been green around the gills when they got him home that afternoon, with a nasty gash that went right down to the bone of his thigh. But he'd taken honey for the shock and his mother had cleaned the wound with salt water, then bandaged it with lint. They'd had many accidents on the farm and she knew what to do. Sure, he'd been worried, he said, but not unduly. Jowen was fit and healthy, used to labouring and stronger than was common. By the time Bray arrived, Jowen, although still in pain, had rallied considerably, was talking quite coherently and sipping water.

"Everyone was confident he'd be back to rights within a couple of weeks, and word had come from the mine he wasn't to hurry back but to take his time. A couple of villagers had been round with baskets of herbs and tonics, and when Joss left the room as Dr Bray arrived, dusk was falling and a candle had been lit. Bray prescribed opium and applied a poultice to the wound, informing the family that should settle matters. Those being his exact words, according to Joss. They'd thanked the doctor for coming as fast as he had, and then left their handsome injured son sleeping peacefully in his bed.

"'I'll never forget his black hair stark against the pillow,' he said. 'Like a raven in snow. Long eyelashes… long and silky just the same as when he was a babe… Peaceful…'

"But he could speak no more. Shook his head, the words choking in his throat. Because what happened next came as a cruel and terrible blow to the Trewhellas. Well, to the whole village. Jowen Trewhella was dead next morning."

"Good God!"

"So that be two young, healthy people dead within weeks of the guldize argument. And that be why we crowders were uneasy."

"But the accident was no one's fault?"

"No indeed, Mrs Quiller. Popular opinion was the lad, distraught by Tamara's sudden death, had been unable to concentrate sufficiently. It was a tragic accident - an explanation that would stand to reason, whilst vindicating those who'd accused the pair of an illicit affair in the first place, proving, if you will, that there'd been a passion between them.

"Then again, one or two folk had stories that didn't fit with that of the doctor on that occasion, either. See, Tristan Bray scribed the medical report to Jowen's employer, Lord Hamlyn, which stated Jowen had died from shock."

"I don't understand," said James. "Joss said he'd rallied when he left him… that he was in pain but talking, drinking water…"

Silas looked into the fire. "Two deaths. Two discrepancies. But Duffy didn't speak out for years, she couldn't, nor had she a hope of contradicting a medical man. And Joss wasn't looking to accuse the doctor, a man who'd come out to help the son who'd wronged him."

"I wonder if Bray was jealous and vengeful enough to overdose them both with opium?"

Silas nodded. "Unquestionably he prescribed opium, but if you'd spoken with Duffy Piper, and then Joss Trewhella, you'd know both young people died with perfectly normal-looking pupils or 't would've been remembered later. That's what I meant a little while ago when I said Tamara's death could have been laudanum poisoning but for one thing, and that was the size of the pupils."

"Oh, I see."

"There was nothing outwardly untoward, see? Which regular man or woman who'd seen Tamara in those final months could attest to the bloodless complexion, bruised eyes and feverish sweating, and swear that wasn't myeloid leukaemia? Even had they noticed pinpoint pupils afore, it had not been the case at death. So it wasn't laudanum poisoning or the eyes would have told the story plain and simple."

"And were they both buried at the church here, the one down the road?" Josie asked.

"Aye, in their family graves. You can see for yourself and check the dates as being within weeks of each other.

"And the good doctor had done his best, a man who'd just lost his most beautiful wife and even tried to help the man who'd cheated him. Tristan Bray had kept his decorum on the night of the guldize, had been humiliated, yet continued to care for his wife and saved the child. No one said a word against him. How could they?

"Had the two young people died with obvious signs of opium poisoning, that may well have been different, but they didn't. The bottle of opium Tristan Bray left in Jowen's bedroom, had barely been touched."

"The Hamlyns? Did they not request more information on Tamara?"

Silas shook his head. "Why would they, Mr Quiller? There was no reason to accuse the doctor of anything untoward. He was trusted, well-liked and respected. He was also the father to their grandchildren. And the little girl, Mary Rose, had miraculously survived due to his skill and care. It was felt blessings should be counted and life must continue, which it seemed to when Tristan and Nancy were wed a couple of months later.

"But then… well, ghosts won't lie still for long if they've something to say… and that's the real story Duffy Piper told us on the quayside that day in Gulston, the reason she and Jan bolted from this house in little more than the clothes they stood up in. And then there was Nancy Peller. Little flaxen-haired Nancy Peller, who, unbeknown to anyone in this village, had a rum reputation afore she turned up 'ere."

***

Chapter Sixteen

"Very pretty, was Nancy – round blue eyes and curly yellow hair – bit on the short side, mind, short and stout. Came from Plymouth way, and folk liked her even afore she saved Mary Rose and brought up the child. Meaner types, or possibly more honest depending on which way you look at it, said she be a bit too fond of her ale. And one or two, those who'd lain sick and alone, said she hadn't been quite as gentle as you'd expect a nurse to be, that she'd another side to her. But that be hearsay. What was not in doubt, though, especially as it be clear for all to see, was Nancy Peller was run so ragged after moving in with Dr Bray and looking after the new baby, as to barely resemble her former self.

"In a very short time, see, she'd gone from plump and round, to the clothes hanging off her bones. She must have thought awful well of the doctor, folks said, to take on another woman's husband, home and children, to be worn that thin within weeks, the weight dropping off her in sack loads. Threw herself into it, she did, devoting herself to him and his motherless children, and still finding time to visit the sick! Used to crochet shawls and blankets for them, fashioning little bracelets and necklaces, very kind, very kind... And by all accounts she made an excellent job of bringing up little Mary Rose, even carrying on long after… Well, there I go, running ahead of myself again.

"Because there's the other child to tell you about first, the little boy, Christopher. You recall he was about two years old and the mirror image of Jowen? Well, to understand what happened, I've to come back to what Duffy Piper told us that day on the quayside. Now Duffy was a woman who hadn't the wits to say anything but what she saw before her, there be nothing other than plain and simple honesty from her, so what she told us I believe and no reason not to. Tamara, she said, was welded to that boy, never let him out of her sight, even paid a photographer to visit and take a picture of just the two of them. Not the husband. Just her and Christopher. That photograph went with the lad later when the Trewhellas took him. Could be they've got it somewhere, and if they have, that would back up what–"

"Took him?"

"Oh, it'd been agreed, Mrs Quiller, the arrangement suiting both parties very well as it turned out. Tristan couldn't stand the sight of Christopher, had never shown the slightest interest in him, but after Tamara's death he made that dislike increasingly clear. Duffy was told to take care of all the boy's needs, something Tamara had insisted on doing herself before Nancy moved in, and not to bother him for anything other than his expenses. Once Nancy became mistress of the house, however, Duffy expected she'd take over. Nancy had been in and out of the house over the past couple of years, she said, always very friendly to Tamara, helpful and kind. But Nancy didn't take over. Instead, one day they were told Christopher would be going to live with the Trewhellas.

"The Trewhellas must've known the truth of the matter between their late son and Tamara, because they took the boy in as their own, and gladly. You'd only to look at the lad, as we said previous, to know he was Jowen's, so maybe there be comfort for them in that? And they'd only girls at the farm, so that's no doubt how it came to suit all concerned. Quiet though, not openly talked about, keeping in mind both the Hamlyns and the Trewhellas were the main employers around 'ere. But it turned out well for Christopher in the end. Strong and handsome like his father, he took to farm work and was brought up as a Trewhella. Imagine that! He'd be Ivy's grandfather, a course."

Josie downed the rest of her sherry and stared into the fire, all the unspoken things she couldn't yet form into words, flaming in the air.

"A very contented man, was Christopher. I had the privilege of meeting him many times. Lived and breathed the land, and not a single day off did he have, not one idle day, and a fair employer, too. So, you see, there wasn't a soul who said the right thing hadn't been done, and that it hadn't worked out well. Not one.

"And so it was for Mary Rose, too. The little girl looked nothing like Jowen or Christopher, but so much like Tristan it couldn't be mistaken. I passed her once or twice when she was out walking with Nancy. Nancy would take her miles – through the woods, across the fields, down the lanes. Folk'd see them both reg'l'r. Small and pale was Mary, with ice-blue eyes set close together, just like him. No doubt about it, the child was in her rightful place as her father's daughter and no one said otherwise. Nancy was a Godsend, and that be the opinion. How she'd put a bad situation right.

"And it be a perfec'ly neat story that would've laid flat

in the church register and quiet inside the pages of a history book but for–"

"But for wagging tongues and silly ghost stories?" Josie said.

"Hang on a minute though, you said Nancy Peller carried on looking after Mary 'even long after' something," James said. "What? Carried on long after what? And what was it about Nancy's reputation? She sounds like a good egg, if you ask me!"

Josie stood up. "It's all something of nothing, tall tales by the fire for those who like a bit of gossip. Want one, Jimmy? Mr Finn?"

James held his glass out for a refill, eyes remaining on Silas. "Is she right? Is it something of nothing? Obviously, there's no such thing as ghosts, lying still or otherwise, I'm adamant on that one; and we've thrown out murder by laudanum. So, apart from the two discrepancies with the doctor's diagnoses, isn't it all's well that ends well?"

Silas nodded. "Could be. But I haven't told you Duffy and Jan Piper's story yet, and as you rightly say, there's Nancy Peller, too. But we'll come to Nancy in a moment and then you can decide what you think, see if your opinion changes. Thing was, Duffy Piper was cruel disturbed by what the doctor said in church that day. She'd been close to Tamara and was very fond of her, took care of her, she said – 'er being little more than a child when she became mistress of the house. And Tamara had confided in her, told Duffy she'd felt pushed into marriage with a man she described as having a heart of granite with regard to womanly charms. Not only that but she was positive Tamara hadn't been ill. There'd been no mention of any diagnoses and definitely not myeloid leukaemia, a term she could neither spell nor pronounce proper. Never heard it mentioned afore. And although Tamara napped during the day, she wasn't by any means struggling with extreme weakness and fatigue, rather she was agitated, restless and frustrated. Seems, and Duffy could still only speak of this in a whisper, Tamara had been hoping to elope with Jowen. Possibly within weeks of the guldize. Except she'd died instead. In fact, so badly upset was Mrs Piper that she saw fit to leave her employment premature. Although that wasn't until after what you asked about, Mr Quiller, which–"

"Were there any medical notes? I mean, I'm a chemist, Mr Finn, and my records and that of our local medics are most meticulous, there must be–"

Silas shrugged. "Ah, that I can't tell ee. But what I meant to say and what you rightly reminded me of was this – that long afore Duffy Piper began to speak of what she saw, indeed long afore she left her employ, Dr Bray lost his mind."

"Really?"

"'Haunted.' Those were his own words, and repeated by Mrs Piper. 'Why the hell won't she leave me alone?' he'd said to her. 'Why the hell won't she stop tormenting me?'

"She'd asked him who. Who wouldn't leave him alone.

"And he'd replied, 'Tamara.'

"This would've been several years after her death. By which time he'd grown most dreadful thin. He'd always been a bony, knobbly sort, but as the months and then years passed, he got thinner and thinner and thinner, 'til his head resembled a skull too big for its frame, the eyes sunken, skin stretched over bones marrow-shiny. He'd not eat, she said, leaving meals untouched. And at night he'd pace around the garden, she and Jan seen him, observing how he'd look up sudden at the bedroom windows, as if he thought someone was there, watching. And for hours he'd sit scribbling furiously at the bureau over there, the one by the window. Went mad in the end, she said. And then one morning he just upped and left. Gone before the sun was up. Vanished. And no one knows where, although a passing farmer supposedly saw him on the road going back up along." He indicated Hounds Tor Lane that led to the rest of the country, just as Beatrice had to Enys a matter of days ago.

"Went back to whence he came, maybe? But gone he most certainly had, and never came back, neither."

"Ghosts again? The ghost of Tamara sent him mad? Good thing Nancy had her head on straight," said Josie. "I expect she was left to bring up Mary and run the house then. To be honest, the more I hear of her the more I admire her, actually."

Silas nodded sagely. "Yes, she stayed to look after Mary. The child would have been about three years old when her father left, and that's no doubt why Nancy was hailed as a saint in this village. Who would bring up another woman's child so selflessly, especially with the husband gone?

"But one or two matters came to light afterwards that I haven't got to yet, see? And none more so than when Jan and Duffy Piper opened up about what happened in that house just afore they scurried off half out of their wits, hot on the heels of Tristan Bray. Things as no one thought to ask, as no one knew, and who could have guessed?

"And then there's Nancy and that reputation."

***

Chapter Seventeen

"Duffy Piper, as I've said before, was an honest soul who'd not wagged her tongue for over three years, and she kept her counsel until she could do so no more. Even then only confiding in the likes of myself and Gil, maybe one or two of those she trusted. But Duffy Piper was a frightened woman. Cruel frightened, she be.

"And see 'ere, there was no denying the state of Tristan Bray's physical appearance or the deterioration of his mind, neither. A lot of people saw him, not just local but all over the county and beyond, including colleagues. And it seemed the doctor was indeed a tormented man. His disappearance was mighty news at the time, reported in the local paper along with the photograph I mentioned earlier. Up 'til then I don't recall his face, see? But an indescribable transformation had come over him, 't was agreed, one that changed the very fabric of his personality. His eyes were hollow sockets, the fetters of death clung to him like a cloak. It was said a room would darken when he entered, that he'd constantly be looking over his shoulder, jittery as a pony at things not there. One or two heard him call out when left alone in a room; his hands shook if a door opened too quickly, and he'd drop whatever he'd been holding – be it cup or glass. He was neither sleeping nor eating, and had taken to sitting up all night. Possibly in the very chair I'm in now, by this same fire.

And then there was the little girl, Mary Rose. Again, this be borne out by others. She'd cry constantly, Duffy said. Nancy took her walking so she'd sleep at night, that be the reason she said, yet still she cried, her little face smeared with tears and everyone seen her. Mary Rose wailed and wailed, never was there a more miserable, tired child. But those who put it down to grief, or even a sour disposition, could not have known what went on inside that house. And that be most likely because they'd never had occasion to experience the inexplicable for themselves. Therefore, to their mind, certain things could not happen. They were not real. And maybe those who did experience that which could not be explained, well maybe they were not able to speak of it at all, for fear of being labelled insane?"

He stared into the flames for a while, before adding, "And things weren't too shiny for poor folk locked up as mad back then.

"But I digress. See, after Tristan Bray had upped and gone, and only Nancy and the tearful, unhappy child were left, matters came to a head. Those days, if you lost your job as a servant then you lost your home, too. And who would employ a servant with a reputation for gossip, especially one spouting tales of ghosts? This be the only reason both Jan and Duffy held their tongues as long as they did. That and how pop'l'r Nancy and the doctor were. Who'd believe them, see? 'Twas only after they'd left and were fortunate enough to secure a cottage over Gulston way, they could tell more of what they knew. And their story was this – that the house became unrestful a few months after Tamara's death, and got progressively worse. Wasn't only Duffy who noticed, neither. It be Jan. And little Mary Rose. And finally, Tristan.

"Initially, it was passed off as a draught or thought to be due to warped wood, but every morning the door to the middle room on the top floor, the one with the round window at the front, would be found ajar. Nancy and Tristan shared the bedroom to the left of that if you stand in the drive facing the house, and Mary Rose had the one to the right. But the middle one had been kept shut after Tamara died, seeing as how the doctor felt it was too upsetting to have to look at her things, and that it had been her favourite room."

Josie's eyebrows shot up to her hairline.

"Nevertheless, each morning that door would be open again. The hinges and brackets were replaced, the window frame examined for draughts, chimney flue swept, but still it swung open every night. The doctor said the door must be warped and a new one was made. Still it swung open. Jan was told to fix this and change that, all to no avail. But with no further rational explanations, there was nothing else to be done. He was beside himself, he said, unable to solve the problem, local craftsmen scratching their heads. In the end it was Nancy who took charge, telling Duffy to store all Tamara's belongings in there, everything that had ever belonged to her, and then Jan was to put a lock on the door. Duffy said Nancy would have had the lot on a pyre but for the doctor's counsel. She wanted nothing of Tamara's left. But Dr Bray felt that Christopher may ask for his mother's things one day, and as such the compromise was made and a lock was–"

"And Mary?" James enquired. "Might Mary not have wanted her mother's belongings one day, too?"

"Indeed, Mr Quiller, and so she might. Thus,

everything was stored and the key turned, the door to remain locked. But would you credit it, a few nights later there that door be, open again. Wide open at half past five in the morning."

"Oh, this is old wives' tales and fanciful nonsense," said Josie.

"And I'd be inclined to agree," James added.

"Aye, but it proved serious for Duffy. She was summoned to explain herself, called dishonest for refusing to admit her failure to lock the door as requested. Fair upset the lady was, and her husband took the Brays' side on the matter too, accusing his wife. He felt his workmanship was being called into question, for how else could it have happened when only Duffy and Tristan had a key? One cast iron key for the housekeeper, one for Dr Bray. But seeing as how it was Dr Bray who'd had the near heart attack when he'd arisen early that morning and found it ajar, it could only have been the housekeeper's fault, could it not? Poor, simple Duffy against the word of the good doctor. She'd been in tears, apparently Nancy's short temper cutting her proper down to size, sharply demanding she explain herself. A course, she could not.

"Now, this happened not just once but many times over, and what followed was this: a specialist carpenter from Gulston was brought in to assess the door fittings and the lock. Nothing untoward was found, and after her dressing-down, Duffy refused, quite sensibly in my opinion, to keep the key no more – ee wanted nothing to do with it lest they accuse her of mischief again.

"But that door would just keep on opening.

"Duffy and Jan lay awake night after night, neither confessing to the other they heard the lock click open.

Duffy took to taking a lamp upstairs, treading gentle and quiet, taking care not to stand accused herself, thinking she might catch one of the family sleepwalking, only to find the door ajar and all three members of the family in bed.

"But Tristan, she said, must have heard the lock click open himself. He went to bed last of any of them, sitting downstairs 'til the early hours in the quiet by the fire. He must've heard that click, then the creak of the boards, followed by what they themselves heard in time – sometimes humming, sometimes the spin and tread of the sewing machine, and sometimes water…water splashing.

"As time went on the atmosphere became uneasy, strained, and Mary Rose had started to wake up in the early hours screaming. Nancy believed it best to leave the child and not to molly-coddle her. Those be her own words. To let her scream and cry herself out. In time she'd grow out of it. But Duffy, who'd none of her own, would go and console her instead. She'd wrap Mary Rose in a blanket and rock her back to sleep. This, she said, went on not just for a few months but for years, and got no better.

"Little Mary Rose, in those bleak hours that precipitate dawn, would tearfully tell Duffy the same thing repeatedly, that a lady was at the wash stand, the one that had been brought out of the middle room, the nursery, for her use. That's what woke her, she said, the lady washing, splashing, and scrubbing. She begged Duffy to take the stand away, but how could she? It was not her place. And so it got worse, and one night when Mary Rose screamed, she told her there'd been a face glaring at her out of the small oval mirror above the basin.

"Duffy told her it was just a dream, but the child was adamant to the last detail, describing a woman she'd never met, could not have known, and of whom there were no photographs, at least not in that house. And this is what sent Duffy Piper's blood running cold. Not only had Mary described her mother, Tamara, but she'd also said the woman had tiny black pins in the middle of her eyes, the face was blue-white and shiny with sweat, and all the skin was scratched off her arms. Now Mary Rose wasn't yet three years old and out of concern for her, Duffy felt it necessary to confide in the doctor. But his reaction sent her reeling.

"He looked shocked, she said, staring at her as if was lying, as if she'd made it all up and had quite lost her mind; before instructing her most sternly to keep the matter entirely to herself, and that he would prescribe Godfrey's Cordial to make sure Mary had no further sleep disturbances. Let that be an end to it! He seemed, she said, most anxious, and absolutely adamant, that the episode never be spoken of again. The syrup was duly administered each night and sometimes during the day, too. And Mary never woke up screaming again.

"Alas, by then the doctor's appearance had begun to tell its own story, as did his increasingly fraught behaviour. That was when he started to pace up and down the garden at all hours of the night, to shout at empty rooms, to suddenly and most violently swing around as if to catch out a pursuer, to address his late wife as if she stood there alive, and spent hour upon hour, Duffy said, scribbling away at that bureau – reams and reams of neat, methodical script.

"Tristan's eyes were wild in those last weeks, Mrs Piper said, the man driven to distraction, hair on end and most unkempt, no longer talking to those of this world; and then he simply upped and left. Never even packed a case; he escaped from the house before anyone else was up. She heard him, though, clear as day, rapid footsteps fleeing down the path as if he was afire with the devil himself in hot pursuit. Jan heard him, too. And that be the first time he spoke to his own wife on the matter. Until then, neither had known the other had heard the ghostly noises, each imprisoned within their own minds, too fearful of standing accused.

"He'd turned to face her, head on the pillow, and said, 'He's gone, then. The doctor's gone. He ain't coming back neither, I'd wager.'

"'What makes you say that?' she'd asked.

"And it was only then he told her about the grave. Afore then, she'd not known a thing about it."

"What grave?" Josie asked.

"Why, the one in the garden, madam."

"Which garden? Not this one?"

"Whose grave?" James asked.

"Aye, this garden, Mrs Quiller. And the grave is Tamara's second child, sir. A baby only a few weeks old – tiny scrap of a thing, a little girl she'd called Enys. Not Mary Rose. And this is why I have to tell you about Nancy Peller."

***

CHAPTER EIGHTEEN

"Good God!" said James.

"This isn't true," said Josie. "Mary Rose looked just like her father, everyone said so, even you!"

"There must have been an inquest, some sort of enquiry when the grave was found?"

Silas shook his head. "The Pipers didn't know what to do. Jan had lived with the horror of what he'd done for years, even keeping it from his wife for fear of what might happen."

"The horror of what he'd done?"

"The baby's body, the one called Enys, was handed to him for secret burial a couple of weeks after Tamara died. And that night Nancy Peller had with her a live child, not more than a few days old. It happened right under their noses, see? But like Duffy, Jan hadn't a devious bone in his body, and so he'd gone and done as asked, taking the explanation as was offered at face value, too affeard of losing the roof over his head to question it. All the same, the affair sat uneasily on his shoulders, and the more he thought about it, the more it weighed him down. Seemed Nancy and Tristan's daughter had smoothly replaced Tamara's."

"There's no proof at all of that," said Josie. "Absolutely none. Just one man's word, and you said yourself, neither he nor Duffy were exactly the sharpest knives in the drawer."

"It's disgraceful," said James. "The whole thing."

"Mary was still the legal heir to the house, though," Josie added. "She's her father's child, at least that's for certain. The other one might not have been."

"Wouldn't that be Christopher?" said James. "He was first born."

"Illegitimate," Josie said. "And besides, he was well provided for by the Trewhellas."

"Er, hang on a minute–"

"That's the conclusion the Pipers came to, Mrs Quiller," Silas said. "By the time Jan confessed to his wife, they both felt in their hearts that the deed had been done. The weak, prematurely born child had died anyway, but both living children were settled and, as you say, well provided for, so might bringing the matter to wider attention make matters worse? Why not let sleeping dogs lie? Besides, who could say whose child truly lay in that grave? Back in those days, how could it be proven, with just the bones left? It would be Jan's word against Nancy Peller's, and he didn't want to take the chance. For some reason the Pipers never disclosed, they both greatly feared Nancy."

James was frowning. "So, hang on a minute. Jan Piper was saying he'd buried Tamara's child? In the bloody garden? The mother in hallowed ground at the church but not the child with her? That makes no sense, at all. Unless… Oh God, I'm being naïve, aren't I?"

Silas nodded. "Unless the hasty marriage to Nancy was for a reason other than to help the good doctor with his burden? P'r'aps their unfortunate situation was neatly resolved with Tamara's demise, and then it all fell conveniently into place? You've to remember how women were disgraced in those days, and that girl, Mary, well she did look uncommonly like her father. It wasn't difficult for them to arrange."

"That's what you meant then, about knowing more about Nancy?" James said.

Silas' eyes flashed. "Folks like me don't forget stories, names or faces, Mr Quiller. And we're partic'l'rly acquainted with the port of Plymouth. And we knows Nancy Peller mighty well, seeing as how we frequent the inns around the docks. Her father was a sailor, see, and her mother… well now…" Here he paused for a moment, selecting his words carefully. "Took in washing while he was away, if you get my drift? Aye, took in washing. Well, young Nancy had a reputation for waiting around the taverns by a young age, looked a lot like her mother – be her double in how she carried on, too." He bared his tombstone teeth. "Taking in washing. Aye, see her regular we did, but that wouldn't be her fault. She made good…

"For a while.

"But here's what I must tell ee. Not long after Tristan Bray left this house, the Pipers fled, too. And they went in a hurry, almost clean out of their wits. What happened on the last day was enough to unnerve them both so bad they couldn't stay another night. They took as many of their possessions as they could, then, in the clothes they stood up in, without a word to anyone, ran down the path and out of here as fast as Dr Bray had not a month before.

"See, not long after he'd told his wife about the grave, Jan was clearing the garden when something happened as was a bit of a shock. The two of them had been talking at night, whispering to each other after Nancy be abed and Mary Rose sound asleep. By then, the child had no appetite at all, sleeping day and night, never made a whimper about any visiting ghost again that can be remembered. Well, after confessing to his wife, Jan began to worry badly about what he'd done, it being impressed on his conscience; and Duffy realised only with hindsight how many fool's errands she'd been sent on the day Enys died and Mary Rose appeared. Nancy had been looking after the baby, see? With her being small and sickly. Nancy had also nursed Tamara, and Christopher. Two dead. One gone.

"Neither could sleep. Both lying wide awake.

"Then a few days later, Jan had been working in a small garden at the back 'ere, one with a patio and an apple tree in the middle, and was cutting back some of the branches when he jumped back as if he'd been bitten. His heart thumped so hard he thought he'd had a heart attack, had to sit down, clutching his chest. It was where he'd buried the baby, see? Buried her underneath one of the stones inside an iron casket. One such as could never be dug up by any wild animal. In his own words he'd made a good job of it. Yet there in front of him lay a tiny human skull, one hollow cavity of the eye staring accusingly up at him from the grass.

"In a terrible panic, he scrabbled over and immediately tugged up the patio stone he'd put on top of the grave, felt down for the casket, praying it still be there. The skull could not belong to the baby he'd buried. It wasn't possible. Couldn't be. But when he pulled it up, to his horror he found the casket empty of the skull, the rest of the skeleton completely intact."

James shook his head. "How?"

"I don't know, Mr Quiller. But, badly unnerved, Jan said he put the head back to where it should be and quickly re-buried it. But as he worked, once or twice he looked up, having the most pressing feeling he was being watched from an upper room of the house. Covered in sweat, he said he was, heart rate ten to the dozen. How in heaven's name had it happened? That's all he could think. To cover it all back up. To pretend it never happened.

"And then a few nights later in the early hours, both heard the key turn in the lock upstairs again, followed by a door creaking open. And after a while, they heard water splashing, just as Mary Rose had described before she was dosed with laudanum. Wide-eyed, they gripped each other's hands. Something unearthly was going on and they admitted to each other they were frightened. That said, they agreed they should check on the child. She no longer screamed, could no longer scream. And so they put their own fears aside and went up…

"Mary Rose, they found fast asleep. But the atmosphere was as charged as if a storm be coming, and the middle door was wide open. Duffy tip-toed along the landing and shut it, unable to explain to herself how, without a key, it could have been opened at all, then went over to the far room and peeped in. Nancy was on her back, softly snoring.

"They returned to their own room together, neither saying a word. Duffy then set the kettle to boil and they lit a fire, sitting up for the rest of the night. They had a ghost, Duffy said, and that's what must have sent the doctor clean out of his mind, and would do the same to them if something wasn't done. Next day Duffy asked Nancy for the key to that middle room so she could lock it herself, and be satisfied it had been done. They didn't want to leave, you understand, they stayed as long as they could. But a short while later, Duffy was upstairs cleaning, alone in the house, after Nancy had taken Mary for one of her long walks. She wasn't unduly concerned about being alone up there with it being broad daylight, but there she was, sweeping the floor, when the door to that locked room swung open right in front of her.

"Riveted to the spot, she stood there with her mouth dropped open, barely able to believe the evidence of her own eyes, when there came the sound of a sewing machine treadle and the whir of a spool. It was a sound she'd once been well used to, as Tamara had liked to do her own sewing, humming quietly as she worked while Christopher lay in his cot in the afternoons; and for a moment it took her sailing backwards in time before she caught herself.

"'Scarborough Fair,' she said it was. Someone was humming, 'Scarborough Fair.'

"It felt very unreal, Mrs Piper said, and her poor heart was thumping dreadful hard, but there it was, the sewing machine ticking over and the door ajar. And there was no denying it. She found she could move neither forwards nor back, was completely paralysed, her head pounding to the beat of her own pulse. And then gradually, almost against her will, she began to walk towards the door.

"There was, a course, no one there; but she felt, then, what she described as a brush of silk against her cheek as she stood on the threshold staring in, and the room was heady with sweet violets – the scent Tamara liked to wear – but sickly and so overpowering her senses reeled. Later, she said she wondered how or even why she did it, maybe to put the ghost to rest, but she remembers wandering into the room, calling out to whoever was there, to what she felt sure was Tamara Hamlyn's spirit. What did she want of her and what could she do?"

"Very brave," said Josie.

"Aye. But no sooner had she entered the room when the door suddenly slammed shut behind her, and in her own words, she became instantly overwhelmed, nay, consumed, by a cloud of darkness, and the shadows closed in. And then without her knowing, with no warning at all, she felt a thud between her shoulder blades and lost consciousness.

"Jan found her eventually, slumped on the floor where she'd fallen.

"They left next day."

"I don't blame them," said Josie.

"No, but Duffy didn't want to leave Mary Rose behind, was extremely concerned about her. She couldn't spend another night in that house though, and in the end she felt Nancy would look after her, especially if her and Jan's suspicions were correct and Mary was actually Nancy's daughter. So the decision was taken to flee, and they were much impoverished by that, so what had either to gain by making such a story up?"

"Indeed," James agreed.

"Ghosts or not, they still can't hurt you," Josie said.

Silas smiled gently. "Let us for a moment assume there be such things as restless spirits, those who remain upon the earthly plane for reasons of love on the one hand or revenge on the other? Unfinished business, should we say? Then might it be possible that if there was a ghost, it was Tamara, and she be angry?"

"I don't think anything terrible had been done, though.

I mean, Mary was still Tristan's daughter and as we said before, both children were provided for. What harm was there really? Enys… oh, I can hardly bear to say that name… but Enys hadn't lived anyway, had she? It was tragic, not really criminal."

James was thoughtful. "It wasn't honest though, was it? And Christopher wouldn't have known who he truly was. So, what happened to Nancy after everyone left? Did she just eventually die of old age?"

"Aye, she passed sometime around the end of the First World War. Liked to frequent The Tailor's Rest a little more often than was seemly, 'er did. She'd tell 'em the liquor helped dull the pain in her bones, and viewing her as being somewhat saintly they cut her some slack, though it be mighty frowned on for a woman to go into a public house on her own. I seen her, mind. I seen her and she seen me. She knew as I knew 'er too, in the woods muttering to herself. Sleep there, I did, on occasion. And ee no more took Mary Rose for long walks for the good of her health, than I bed down in a four poster and silk sheets every night. What ee did do though, was go chant into that pisky well, draw signs on stones and trees, and ee knew her henbane from her hemlock."

"Henbane… visions…?"

Silas nodded. "Aye, Mr Quiller. But by the time Mary Rose was grown, Nancy be bent double, had to walk with two sticks, and her spine so crooked and hunched it be pitiful to see. And then one afternoon, round about dusk when one of the farmhands be returning from the fields, there she lay in a crumpled heap of sticks and rags on the lane. That misfortune of the spine, of the bones, runs in her family, see? Nancy's mother had the very same problem only it took her premature, and I remember most clearly and most partic'l'r, just as yesterday, the day she collapsed in much the same manner. There's only us travellers who'd 'ave known, see?

"Tis obvious now, should a person know to look, that Mary Rose was never Tamara's child, seeing as how Mary Rose turned out later down the line, bent double just like 'er. She was quick-tempered like Nancy, too. Oh aye, snap your head off they would, soon as look at you, that flash of the eyes hard as flint. Made folks wonder if it be the same person they'd spoke to a moment afore. No doubt in my mind, or anyone else who knew them - Mary was a Peller, not a Hamlyn.

"And that, Mr and Mrs Quiller, was what I meant about Nancy.

"But as for proving all that..." He shrugged. "As the Pipers said, maybe it's best to let sleeping dogs lie? Christopher's descendants, just like Mary's, have all been well looked after."

"That's what I said," Josie agreed. "It's all hearsay, nothing provable. Doesn't help anyone, opening up a can of worms like that, does it? And Doctor Bray isn't here to defend himself, either."

"Indeed, Mrs Quiller. Unless you're wont to listen to ghost stories, and then it be a different matter altogether–"

"Which I'm most definitely not."

"No, Mrs Quiller. I can see that."

Josie finished her sherry and glanced at the clock. "Good grief! Three hours have gone. I can't believe it. Well, it was quite a yarn, Mr Finn, and good to know our history even if it's... well... colourful." She yawned. "Bedtime for us, I think, but look – you haven't even touched your drink."

"Ah, but I will now, Mrs Quiller. I will now."

"Have a mince pie," James said, proffering the plate. "I'll join you. What about a slice of Christmas cake?"

"Thank ee kindly, sir. Thank ee... And then I'll say goodnight and a very happy Christmas to you. And to the little girl – Enys, isn't it? If she remembers me, that is."

Josie stood up and smoothed down her skirt. "I'm sure she will. Thank you so much for coming. It's certainly been an interesting evening, quite a revelation, if a somewhat disturbing one."

"All a very long time ago," said Silas, reaching for his cap. "And I expect we'll never really know the full story about Tamara. Well, not unless the doctor's notes surface."

"If Doctor Bray was guilty of anything he'd have burnt those, I expect," said Josie.

"If he had any sense," said James.

Silas stood up and held out his hand. "I bid you goodnight, thank ee kindly for the hospitality, and I wish you both well in your new home."

"Oh, we're not staying," said Josie, leading him into the hallway. "We're from London. We're going to sell the house. I couldn't settle here."

She opened the door and a sheet of freezing air wafted in.

"Probably just as well," said Silas. "Imagine if you and your child had been murdered, your beloved son ousted and your home passed to the murderer's mistress who poisoned the husband with henbane until he fled quite insane, leaving everything to her and her own child – the one who may or may not have been begotten deliberately, to encourage an embittered man to commit terrible deeds.

Imagine just for a minute that be true.

"Be enough to make a restless spirit very angry indeed, I'd say. You'd haunt the place, wouldn't you? Could be the lady won't rest until the truth be found and the wrong be righted. No, I wouldn't want to stay here, either. But that's just me and my ilk… we believers in the unseen, in spirits, magic and strange stories… Anyway, I'll bid ee goodnight. Merry Christmas, Mrs Quiller, Mr Quiller."

Josie closed the door quickly behind him, leaving the outside lantern on so he could find his way to the lane.

"Brrr! What a strange man! And wasn't it funny how the time slipped away? It was like he'd only been here five minutes, I…" On noticing James's face she stopped mid-sentence.

He was frowning.

"What's the matter?"

He marched to the door and flung it wide. "I didn't hear…"

They both looked out at a sheet of pristine virgin snow sparkling with crystals of frost. Absolutely unblemished. The night sky was studded with stars, the air glacial. A few yards away, picked out by the moonlight, was a line of small, very deep prints from the back door to the barn, made earlier by Enys.

They turned to face each other. The thought the same, the words unspoken. There were no footprints leading to or from the front door. Unless Silas Finn had levitated or vanished into thin air, it was as if he'd never been.

***

Part Three
Enys Quiller

'The darkness always lies'
Anthony Liccione

Chapter Nineteen

I'd been eavesdropping on the stairs, clutching the bannisters, when I heard their voices rise and shot up to my room before I was caught. The moment is a clear, bright shard in my memory, and that's how I know for a fact, without any doubt whatsoever, that Silas Finn vanished into thin air.

I'd gone straight to the bedroom window to watch him walk down the drive. I made it even before the sound of their goodbyes echoed in the flagstone porch, and well before the door latch closed behind him. So, I know. There is no mistake. The shock is not something I've ever forgotten – the front door was opened, they all said, 'Goodnight, Merry Christmas,' and then the droll teller was outside in the yard.

Except he wasn't. There was no one there.

The snow had stopped falling hours before. It lay like frosted white icing on a cake, glittering and still. There wasn't a breath of wind to whirl away the crunchy sugar coating, no sheen of rain or hovering mist to obscure the scene. Beneath a sharply clear sky and a full moon, you could see all the way up to the stone circle and beyond, certainly to the end of the drive and the steely ribbon of the lane as it tapered down to the valley. There wasn't a sound out there, the only visible track the one I'd made earlier. I stared and stared at the pristine snow, until the evidence before me could be denied no longer: there were no footsteps leading to or from the front door of the house.

But he existed! I'd sat on the stairs listening to the droll teller's story through the gap in the living room door for over two hours, with the chattering teeth and frozen feet to prove it. I couldn't make sense of it at all, was so stunned, so shattered, I think I must have simply crawled into bed and blanked it from my mind.

Certainly I said nothing about it for a very long time, years and years. Partly, there was the worry of being scolded, but perhaps the greater fear was not being believed, labelled deluded, fanciful, mad. How could I explain it? The whole thing sounded ridiculous, and the more time that passed, the more incredible it seemed. I could already hear the responses – 'Enys, there are no ghosts, they do not exist, you have to stop this, you've been listening to silly stories and it's gone far enough.' They'd say I'd fallen asleep, then gone to the window after the snow had covered his prints. Yet it was not snowing when he left. For hours it had not snowed. The sky was clear and remained so all night.

So, I told no one about the vanishing storyteller. And for a long time I told no one about seeing Tamara's ghost again, either. Not after that first night. What was the point? But I had seen her, and I knew my mother had, too. She lied to me. They both lied and they kept on lying. Because ghosts did exist and they knew it. And I had a suspicion that, just like the droll teller said, the one at Gorse Bank House not only existed but was angry.

Could be the lady won't rest until the truth be found and the wrong be righted.

The absolute truth, though, without any biased perspective, can be a strange and elusive thing; and in the end turned out to be about as far removed as it was possible to be, from anything even the droll teller had surmised. And it was nothing like anything I'd expected, or even knew existed.

But back to that night... As I'd sat gripping the bannisters, limbs frozen to icicles, hugging myself to keep the blood flowing, I'd submitted to the magic of the story, my head a confusion of disconnected names, places and emotions. It was only afterwards, when I tried to make sense of it all, that I remembered with a stab of panic, that Beatrice had to be told directly what was said. The thought woke me up a few hours later. It couldn't be vague, I had to remember!

Although Silas Finn had spoken in a thick Cornish brogue, he'd made every effort to be understood by both parents, my dad in particular, which meant I'd understood it too, of course. Well, most of it. The significance of some aspects only registered years later, but I processed more than enough at the time, particularly the part that had caused me to slap a hand over my mouth. It was when Silas Finn said Jan had buried Tamara's baby in the garden, a dirty secret thrown away and forgotten. And that the baby's name was Enys.

Enys... Enys...

Those ghostly whispers. Meant for me? Or another Enys from long ago? Why my name? Why? The impact hit me hard, had felt shockingly personal. What a terrible thing to have buried her out there in the garden, her life snuffed out, replaced by another more important child, to lie completely unacknowledged in the dirt, to rot, unloved, discarded…

And so when I woke up, remembering the story, what had been uppermost in my mind was the abandoned buried baby. I clung to the spirit of her, the idea of her, as to a strand of cotton. Somehow, reeling in that thread, discovering what was at the end, would solve everything, relieve all the confusion, stop my own reality unravelling. I don't think I'd ever felt truly alone like that before. My parents would leave her in the ground, of that I was sure. A nonsense, silly story. In one more day we were due to leave, they would sell the house and justice would never be done. Perhaps that's why I did what I did? I don't know. I was ten.

I'd be glad if you told me dreckly, what the real story is, because he's the only one who'll know… So, make sure to ask him, won't you? When he says story or song?

What I was not aware of back then, however, was that both parents, in their different ways, had been deeply disturbed by the droll teller's visit. Perhaps even more than I was.

Next morning was Boxing Day, and Mum was clattering around in the kitchen, already packing, making shopping lists for when we got back to London. She couldn't wait to leave, and with hindsight it's obvious why. The atmosphere was fractious and she was talking like the clappers, with no room for a word in edgeways from anyone else. I'm sure she'd explained Silas Finn's story very neatly to herself, had compartmentalised the parts she may need to mould and rationalise, and had no intention of ever acknowledging the rest. Could be she'd asked herself what the point would be? All were catered for. What good would it do to rake over the ashes of an old family drama? And she could have been right. For her, it was right.

But it wasn't right for me and it wasn't for my dad, either. He was stewing. Oh God, you could see it all over his face. He wore his disquiet like a lead hat. It visibly weighed down his shoulders, haunting his eyes, tipping chin to chest, and furrowing his brow. I didn't know at the time, had I been older I'd have guessed, but what was eating away at him, what plagued his mind and kept him awake after hearing that story, was murder! While my mother's main concern was inheriting the house and selling on as soon as possible, and mine was the forgotten baby in the garden, he was thinking about medical notes and record-keeping, about proof. It bugged him immensely. So much so, he clearly wasn't thinking about the consequences of his actions, but I'll come to that later because a couple of catalytic things occurred that day to compound matters.

The first being a surprise visit from Beatrice Trove.

She turned up just after breakfast. Dressed in a navy duffle coat and wellies, she stood outside the porch, fresh-faced and rosy-cheeked, green eyes a-glitter, bearing a tin of Christmas cake and mince pies for our journey home.

"Very kind," my mother said, not asking her in.

"And thank you for my present, Auntie Josie," Beatrice said. "I love rose-scented things."

Mum had palmed her off with soap from Dad's shop, and something inside deflated a little because of the white lace tights I'd been given. Ivy must have made a special trip to town just to please me, and Beatrice had clearly inspired her to do it.

"That's all right. So, did you have a good night last night? Barn dance go well, did it?"

"Oh yes, we were up 'til midnight. The Hamlyn boys

came over from the House –Mark and Henry. And the fiddlers are still there, well, all except the old man, but he slipped away at dawn." She glanced at me. "Did anyone come over to you then, for a story or a song?"

My heart did a little flip with the directness of the shot, sudden and unexpected, and any attempt at a reply stuck in my throat.

But while I was floundering, my mother stepped in seamlessly, and did something that sent a shockwave, a little bolt of electricity, straight through me. She looked Beatrice in the eye and said, "No. We saw no one."

Beatrice turned to me then, and I saw in her face, as she saw in mine, that we both knew it was a big fat lie. My cheeks began to burn as my dad's footsteps sounded on the flagstones behind us.

"Really?" Beatrice said loudly. "How funny, because–"

"Anyway, we must press on now, Beatrice. I'm glad you're pleased with your present and do thank your mother for the cakes, won't you? I was worried the shops wouldn't be open, and what with barely a tin of corned beef left in the cupboards at home..."

"Yes, I will, Auntie Josie." Then, just as Dad joined us at the door, she added, "Can Enys come out and play snowballs? Oh, please, Auntie Josie. We might not see each other again for years! We'll be ever so good."

I had a yearning then, it overcame me, so powerful as to have already taken flight. And before my mother could object I'd pulled on my boots and grabbed an anorak.

Her words, "All right, but no more than ten minutes..." trailed behind us as we ran into the blinding-white, crisp morning air.

I was going to find that grave, and not only that – I was

going to tell Beatrice everything Silas had said.

***

CHAPTER TWENTY

I knew exactly where to look and headed straight for it.

"Are we going somewhere partic'l'r?" Beatrice asked, as we rounded the corner of the house at speed.

"Yes. Hurry!"

"Where?"

"You'll see." I picked up pace, crossing the lawn. "Come on, we haven't got long."

"He did come, didn't he?"

"Yes."

"Why'd she lie?" She picked up a snowball and it hit me in the arm. "They be watching from the kitchen window. Throw one back!"

We ran then, breathless and squealing, exhilarated by the clean, icy whiteness; and by the secret, that this time I was the one to hold, the one who was bursting to tell.

To this day, I find it incredible my mother never suspected I'd been on the stairs listening in, and odder still that she'd sat and heard the droll teller out. She hadn't wanted to, anyone could see that, afraid perhaps of what he might say? But then sometimes when I'm alone, in a moment caught off-guard, I find myself dropping back into that pocket of memory, to the drawn-out strings of his violin as firelight leapt around the walls, to the vibrations echoing through the chambers of the heart, to the craving, the insatiable desire, to possess hidden knowledge. And to carry on listening to the story, to observe it playing behind the shutters of the eye long after it became macabre and ghoulish. Inconvenient. Long, long after I hadn't wanted to. There'd been a certain magic, something otherworldly, and there's an excellent chance I'll never know how he did it.

"Did you find out what happened? What did he say?"

"Yes." We were running towards the boundary wall, continuing to throw the odd snowball. "Have they gone from the window?"

She screamed especially loudly, and fell dramatically, head back for a clear view of the house. "Yeah, can't see anyone."

"Come on then." I headed for the arched gate in the wall. "Follow me."

"Tell me quickly!"

We hurried down the path to the small garden with the apple tree in the middle of the patio. "I was sent out," I said over my shoulder, "made to go to bed, but I listened on the stairs. They got rid of me when he started talking about Tamara Hamlyn, and how she'd had an extra-marital something or other with Jowen Trewhella–"

We'd arrived at the tree, where I stopped and crouched low. She crouched next to me and we spoke then in hurried whispers. Beatrice knew exactly what extra-marital meant, and was nodding knowingly. "This is a good garden, sheltered all round. Come on, tell me."

I told her then, as fast as possible, all I'd heard and could rightly remember.

"We knew about Jowen, already. Great-grandad Christopher told my mother he died just after the doctor visited, yet all he'd had was a gash on the leg. He'd been sitting up and talking, lost quite a bit of blood, but should have been perfec'ly fine, that they'd seen worse accidents on the farm. But then Doctor Death came over and he be stone dead by morning. A course, no one could prove a thing. What could they do?"

I remembered that bit and nodded, not understanding how it could have happened either, while with a dull thud it hit me that part of the droll teller's story, at least, was true. Then, with no time to lose, and constantly checking over my shoulder, I rapidly filled her in on the rest. And when I'd finished, I looked down at the stones beneath our feet, and said, "So, I think the real baby was buried here – Tamara's baby – the one replaced by Mary Rose that no one knew about."

"Enys?"

"Yes. Enys."

The moment Silas Finn had told my parents about baby Enys was the moment the swirling kaleidoscope of my world had refused to settle down again, not ever, not into any pattern. It had cast me adrift on an ebbing tide of abandonment, as if the unwanted child was me, and that feeling had stayed, of floating away.

Beatrice was staring at my face. I could feel the heat coming off her in waves. "So, let me get this correc'ly… Doctor Death bumps his wife off, bumps Jowen off, then 'im and Nancy Peller swap Tamara's dead baby for their own? And Nancy had a spine deformity that only showed up in old age, just like Mad Mary's did? Add in the temper and 'er talking to piskies in the woods. This could make sense of everything. Don't you see? This could prove the lot!"

The twisted charcoal branches of the apple tree were grey with lichen and iced with snow, but there in the shelter of the walled garden, just visible, were small blossom buds pushing through; and beneath it, close to the trunk, snowdrops and crocus bulbs had already started to sprout, green and fresh. I stared down at them, recalling how Jan Peller had been cutting back the bare, spiky branches that day, when he'd found himself looking down at a tiny unearthed skull – one he had personally, secretively, buried beneath the stones, had kept quiet about in order to keep his job and his home. How his heart must have leapt in his chest. I pictured him ashen, eyes out like organ stops, pulse roaring in his ears as he stumbled back to the house.

"So he put the bones back into a casket? Here? Under one of these stones?"

I struggled to remember exactly what had been said, there'd been so much. How Silas Finn had recalled all that detail was a question I hadn't thought to ask, a story carried for all those years and not a scrap of it lost.

"I think so. One of the stones, he said. I don't know exactly where, but I know it was the apple tree and the patio, and he'd thought someone was watching from the house, so…"

We both looked up at the house, the only window overlooking us being one of the rear bedrooms on the upper floor.

"One way to find out." She ran a gloved finger around the edges of the stones, feeling for signs of leverage. "We've been ages already. Come on, help me find it. With a bit of luck they'll be busy doing something else and forget about us."

I think we both expected to see one of them, or both,

striding up the path at any moment, demanding to know what the hell we were doing. But the miracle was that we found it. I sometimes find it hard to believe that we did, and so quickly, too. But one of the stones had a small amount of give.

"Help me, come on. What can we use to prise this up with? Don't you see? Don't you see how important this could be?"

I looked around, remembering the rusty table with a trowel on top of it. "I know!"

A minute later we were levering up the stone. But just before we pulled it back, I looked into those eyes of hers, sea green, no longer dancing with mischief but glittering hard as jewels.

"You ready for this?" she said, as her fingers curled around the top and she began to tug, to wrench it free, the wool of her gloves grimy with muddy snow.

I could barely speak, could only nod. Somewhere deep inside, a fleeting spark of hope fired up, that if there was anything there it would be a family pet interred out of love, out of care... and not a discarded baby, buried for an altogether different reason. Silas had the story mixed up, a rumour twisted and changed in the re-telling, an added fabrication of grotesque proportions. But maybe an even deeper part of me didn't want anything to be there for another reason – that the droll teller's account could be true.

There was a sudden give, a sigh of air, and then Beatrice fell backwards with the stone still in her hands. Before I'd even had chance to look into the chamber, however, she'd scrambled forwards, reached down, and pulled something out.

We both stared at it agog. A small iron casket. It may once have been used to keep something airtight, but it was too old, too rusty, to identify. She glanced at me briefly, before fumbling for the catch on the side. All I could do was watch, sitting back on my haunches, as the inevitable unfolded and it sprang open like a trap.

Inside was a waddle of rags, which she feverishly unwrapped, layer by layer like a Russian doll. My heart rate was escalating, every anxiety, every fear, every nightmare, rising like bile, to stick in the gullet, where it lodged, paralysing my throat, my mouth. And when she'd finished, the truth was laid bare. A tiny human skeleton, perfectly preserved.

How in this world had Jan Peller found it on the grass that day? What a hellish shock that had to be. For how could that stone have been moved and replaced, unless purposefully? How could that casket have been opened and put back minus the head? Unless it was deliberate? How? The words, the thought, that someone had wanted to scare the crap out of the only living witness, did not occur to me then, of course. All I was aware of was the intense, Arctic cold and Beatrice's searching eyes as we looked at each other and comprehension sank in – Silas Finn's story now carried weight.

"It could belong to any baby, though," I said eventually.

"Yes, imagine what story they told Jan Piper! Happen, it belonged to one of Tristan Bray's patients, a woman in the village who wanted it kept a secret," she agreed. "But if this wasn't Tamara's, then how come the one that went on living looked nothing like her, let alone Jowen? And I mean, nothing like her, not one family trait. Yet was supposed to be hers, the legit one between her and Dr Death, and the only reason he was allowed to continue living here? Oh, you don't know about that? The house was for Tamara and her descendants! And you haven't seen a picture of Tamara's other child, Christopher, have you? I'll tell you what a child of hers looked like."

She narrowed her eyes, holding tightly onto the bundle as if what was inside remained alive and needed to be kept warm.

Clouds heavy with snow had blown over the sun, and a raw chill spread then across my back, the sweat from our frantic endeavour rapidly cooling. I shook my head, shivering, fixated on the mess beneath the tree, the gaping hole and dislodged stones. What was Beatrice going to do? She was talking about house deeds and rightful heirs. I didn't understand a word except trouble was coming. What would happen to me?

"He had thick, black, curly hair and wide brown eyes," she said, getting to her feet. "He was broad-chested and well-built like all the Trewhellas, but with her beauty added in. He was an extremely handsome man, Enys Quiller."

I trailed behind as she hurried back down the path, my turn to ask where we were going, what she was going to do, to tell me.

"That's the thing, see?" she said, breathless, as we marched across the grass. "Mad Mary looked like Doctor Death, who Tamara was forced to marry on account of there being no one else the family approved of. No one else good enough. The fact he was ugly with close-together eyes and a mouth like an upside-down spoon, didn't stop them making her marry him. And now, on top of that, you're saying that nurse of 'is was a traper from Plymouth docks, as well as being a pisky wi–"

"Traper?"

"Slut! Just wait 'til my mother hears this! Funny how both Tamara and Jowen had to die, wasn't it? So quick after the guldize when Doctor Death be made a fool of? Your mother's a cuckoo in the nest, Enys Quiller, and this proves what folks always thought."

A shard of fear glanced through me like a sheet of ice, and as we neared the house again, I noticed how dark the windows were. A sudden gust of wind scattered snowflakes across the lawns. What had I done? Oh God, what had I done?

Beatrice picked up speed on her cross-country-runner legs, gripping the incriminating bundle.

I couldn't keep up.

"Where are you going?" My voice sounded tiny and inconsequential, lost in the vastness of everything, my mouth frozen, ears throbbing, fingers and toes numb. I was wet –wet and cold, miserable, nose dripping. "What are you going to do?"

She had her back to me, stomping in and out of the snow, and didn't reply.

"It wasn't Mary's fault," I called out. "Or my mother's."

She only turned round after reaching the drive, when the lane was in sight. "True."

"Your family's provided for," I said, breathless, repeating verbatim my mother's words from the night before. "Let sleeping dogs lie."

I didn't even know what that meant.

She said nothing.

And then words that were mine and mine alone, that

emanated from a well deep inside, burst out. "You have a beautiful home, one I'd have liked. You have everything. You have horses and the beach and the fields and dogs and… and… everything…" I was blinded by tears that wouldn't hold back.

Still she said nothing.

Bleakness howled all around, an ill wind from every direction, as my mother's shadow loomed over me as darkly as the house that silently observed us, its windows snow-reflected hollows. Already I was living the stony silence of tomorrow's journey home.

"My mum had to leave here and work very hard. Don't do this. Maybe we should just put the baby back instead of upsetting everyone?"

But my heart was not in the words and thus carried no power. We both knew we would not be doing that. To this day I can see the open grave and the rusty trowel beneath the tree. Can still see the heavy stones we levered up, the grimy snow smeared across the patio. There was no way we could simply put all that back and walk away. What had been done had been done.

"Those ghosts won't rest though, will they, Enys Quiller?" she said, more softly than I'd expected. "Not until this wrong be righted. And whoever this baby may be, they deserve a proper respectful burial. Don't you think?"

With that I couldn't argue.

And so I watched her walk purposefully and quickly towards the lane. She did not look back; and for a long time afterwards I found I couldn't move.

All that could be heard was the rushing of the wind off the wintry moors, and all that could be seen was the whiteness for miles and miles and miles, a glare that merged with the blanched sky.

What the hell was she going to do? That was all I could think. What the hell was Beatrice going to do?

***

Chapter Twenty-One

Ivy Trove took the baby's bones straight to Victor Hamlyn.

I was not to know that, however, until many more years had passed. All I knew was one hell of a storm was coming. Like a wild animal I sensed it, felt the icy ruffle of hairs on the nape of my neck, and the heightened energy in the air.

But the storm was not to break for a few weeks. The discovery alone proved almost nothing in the absence of further evidence, especially not in those days. I didn't know that, of course. Instead, for a long time after Beatrice had gone, I stood rigid and freezing in the drive, with visions of her bursting into the farm kitchen, thrusting the baby's bones into Ivy's arms, telling her my mother was 'a cuckoo in the nest.' We had no right to be here and we didn't belong, that's what Ivy and Beatrice would say. We belonged nowhere. I did not understand the consequences, not at all, except they were coming, and were serious.

Yet in my heart I loved the place beyond expression, the thought of leaving it making me almost sick with grief. And I remembered those dreams that weren't dreams – the love in Tamara's eyes had been more real than anything I'd ever known, the bond a lifeline thrown down through the ages, one that wrapped and twisted around my heart.

Enys...Enys...

But there was another catalytic thing that happened

that day. One that temporarily took my mind clean off Beatrice as soon as I walked back in the house.

Neither parent had come to find us, had they? And we'd been gone a long time. That struck me as peculiar long before I stirred myself from the statue-like shock in the drive. A wet, icy wind had been battering at my back, wailing and whistling in my ears, sleety rain had whipped my face stinging raw, and the sombre low clouds over the moors were rolling in with more snow.

Yet they hadn't come to find me.

The house was unnaturally quiet.

I stood dripping on the flagstones in the hall when a horrible possibility took hold of me, that they could be dead. They were both lying dead on the bed upstairs, eyes staring glassy and unseeing at the ceiling, skin ghastly grey, bodies with no one inside… I was alone, completely alone, would be alone forever…

"Mum? Dad?"

The stairs creaked as warily I made my way upstairs. Which was where I found them, sitting in the middle of the floor in the room with the round window.

"Probably he burnt them," my mother was saying.

"Why would he do that if he'd nothing to hide?"

"Well, I don't know, do I? Jimmy, what's the point of all this? It benefits no–"

Their voices had been low, scarcely above a hiss, and they both jumped when first one, then the other, became aware I was standing in the doorway.

The whispery conversation faltered only slightly though, and they quickly resumed it as if I wasn't there. Had never been there. Was, in fact, invisible.

My dad had been convinced medical notes existed, even

in the late nineteenth century. He'd worked with many physicians during his twenty-year career to date, and dates, symptoms, histories, diagnoses and treatments, were always, he said, recorded. His own were in the form of separate cards for each patient, filed in wooden drawers at the back of the shop. Tinctures, syrups, tablets, powders and ampoules, were all dutifully logged to protect both practitioner and patient, but also to aid the memory of the busy practitioner and inform colleagues. Had there been misdeeds regarding Tristan Bray's conduct, he reasoned, there would be written evidence of that somewhere. Or maybe a significant portion of notes would be glaringly omitted?

My mother's voice was loaded with exasperation. "Perhaps he took anything incriminating with him, then?"

Maybe it would have been better for all of us if he had? Or burnt them, like she said.

"At least let me look!"

Turned out my father had already broken into the bureau and had some of the floorboards up downstairs, finding nothing but dust and spiders. And it also turned out he was far more determined to get to the root of the matter than any of us thought. Perhaps he wanted to settle his own mind, to convince himself there'd been no murder, no foul play? Or had it run deeper, and been about Silas Finn? If he could prove the story was rubbish, with no foundation, he could forget the whole thing. I don't think even he knew the answer to that. But he was absolutely single-minded, resolute; you could say obsessed.

"You can't build a house on quicksand," he kept saying. "One day it'll come crashing down on top of us. It will!"

The locked bureau in the lounge had been empty, just

as my mother told him it would be. It was a wooden roll-top desk positioned to overlook the garden, from which Tom Hamlyn, as co-executor with the solicitor in Gulston, had retrieved Mary's formal papers. All it had contained were receipts, bank account and solicitor details, a ration book yellow with age, and a very full diary of the shrubs, trees and flowers planted in the garden, complete with a meticulous map of where they were. There had been nothing reflecting a personality, no correspondence with others, no photographs, not even a mention of her father or mother, let alone daughter. It was almost, Tom told my mother at Mary's funeral, as if the memory of them had been wiped clean. But probate, he said, shouldn't be a problem: Mary had bequeathed everything to Josephine Quiller, and if she wanted to sell the house it could be done expediently as Victor Hamlyn would purchase privately. Gorse Bank House would, he'd apparently said, round off their estate nicely. It could be restored at long last. They were looking forward to it.

In short, it was a fait accompli. In my mother's mind she'd already hightailed it back to London, purchased a much bigger house with the proceeds and given up her job.

I think Dad must have been so close to agreeing to that, would love to have done, but after the visit from Silas Finn he was not himself, and she was powerless to prevent him conducting a frenzied search of the place. They wouldn't get another chance, he said. He had to quiet his mind on the matter, do all he could. She was just to let him look, to at least try to find the facts. He felt sure no one could have thought to do so before. Who else had the full story, but us? And who else had the opportunity to search for conclusive proof, let alone know what to look for? Mary, he said, had sat on this for ninety years. Ninety years!

Events felt as if they were tearing along at an alarming pace, and just as I'd been hellbent on finding the grave, so my dad was with those medical notes. Silas Finn's work was done, it seemed. All the restless spirit had to do now was wait, safely assured history would now unravel, spinning ever faster down to the bare bobbin of truth. And nothing could stop it.

My mother was visibly irritated, fingers digging into her palms, as Dad stood in the centre of that middle room, raking his hair back and forth, staring around him at the piled-high boxes. A violent gust shook the walls, as the ominous clouds I'd seen on the moors rolled over the house. Soot blew down the chimney.

"I just want to make sure before we leave, that's all. Once we've gone the house will be cleared and sold, and we'll never know what happened. Don't you want to know if Tamara was your real great-grandmother, Josie? Or if she was murdered?"

"You're not buying into all that nonsense, are you? No. No, I don't. And it was so long ago, I fail to see why you should be so bothered, either. Just stop this madness, Jimmy. Why are you so obsessed?"

I wanted him to stop, too. What was he thinking? Why couldn't he just leave it? Mum was right – we should just go. I bit my lip, wishing we could, that day, that minute; and I couldn't stop myself from repeatedly glancing out of the window, expecting Beatrice and Ivy to come marching up the drive with a bundle of bones in their arms, half the village in tow… A mob with torch flames, or more likely police vans… Mutely, I felt for the wall behind and tried to quell the fear. What had I done? What would my dad find?

Would they send me somewhere? Send me away when they knew what I'd done?

But like I said, I could not have known just how thoroughly Silas Finn had unnerved him. Nor did I have the faintest idea that the night before, while I slept, exhausted, he'd heard the lock to the middle room click open. My mother had been asleep beside him, and so he hadn't woken her, but got up to close the door again, turned the key in the lock, and then returned to bed. When he awoke again, however, my mother wasn't there. Recounting the story years later, he said he thought it was about two in the morning, and for a while he'd lain still, expecting to hear the toilet flush, followed by the pad of feet hurrying back along the landing; but there wasn't a sound.

After a few more minutes had passed, he got up to find the door to the middle room ajar once more. Only this time my mother was inside, sitting on the window seat gazing out at the moonlit lane. Frozen to the bone, she was humming to herself, the room heady and sickly with an overwhelming scent of violets.

Just as I had done a few nights before, he led her back to bed, but then lay stark awake, his mind drifting over all Silas Finn had said, unable to explain why his own daughter had screamed she'd seen a ghost, then described the same one Mary Rose had to the housekeeper all those years ago – right down to the incessant washing, the deathly pallor of the face, and the scratched arms. How was it possible Silas Finn had known that? And how was it he could recall everything in so much detail, a story from ninety years before?

I see now he'd been truly haunted, absolutely shaken to

the core of his existence; at stake all he thought was real and true, solid, safe and explicable.

So, when he looked into her eyes and tersely replied, "Well, perhaps it's called a moral compass," it jarred us both, mother and daughter.

All we could do was observe helplessly then, as he set about scouring the room, taking down boxes, rifling through contents, until he either found what he was after, or was forced to concede there was nothing more to be done. And so, like the sight of Beatrice purposefully stomping up the lawn with the baby's bones in her arms, there was a feeling of leaden inevitability. There was, however, a lot to get through, and he quickly became heated in the face, sandy hair flopping onto a forehead shiny with sweat, and all the while my mother was leaning against the doorway watching. He'd find nothing, she kept saying. Nothing. This was ludicrous, he'd gone completely mad, they ought to be packing, it'd be dark soon.

I clearly remember staring at the faded green wallpaper and how the corners were peeling, my nerves jarring afresh at the sight of a jack-in-the-box and a crocheted shawl pulled from one of the crates, although I couldn't say why. All I could think was my mother would never forgive him for this, that everything was unravelling, picturing that spool whirling ever faster, to the drum pedal of an old sewing machine, less and less cotton to shield us from the bare horror of what I knew, deep down, was coming.

And then only the chest was left. The light was fading, defeat weighted his shoulders, and I had my fingers crossed behind my back, praying Ivy wasn't coming. That we might leave tomorrow. Nothing would happen about that baby. No one would know I dug it up. I could get away with it. Why had I done it, though? Why? I had no idea, except I'd felt there was no choice, that's about the best explanation I can give – that I was compelled. Perhaps that's what happened to my dad, too?

Extraordinarily heavy, the chest had to be dragged away from the wall, walked inch by inch, until it was positioned below the bare light bulb in the middle of the room, where the lid could be opened fully and the contents clearly seen. You could almost sense the restless spirits of the past gathering around to watch the show, feel the collective sigh of anticipation.

The renewed hope I'd had weakened a little then as, with a chill premonition, I went over to sit on the window seat, sleet spattering on the glass behind. He'd find what he was looking for in there, the voice inside me said. He was going to find it in there…

It was an old-fashioned mahogany trunk made in the Far East, lacquered and ornately carved, with a brass lock fashioned with a long pin requiring a particular kind of key. Of course, that key had long gone. And nothing was budging despite his best efforts.

"Damn! I'll have to hack it off," he said grimly.

"Oh, for goodness' sake, you can't do that. Come on now, Jim. Enough's enough. It's just an old sea chest. Look, you can see the stickers, and the light's going now, we really ought to…"

But her words sailed over his head and he didn't hear them. No longer in harmony with each other, neither received the other's thoughts or tuned into the other's emotions, their focus now on totally different trajectories.

"I'll get that old tool box out of the garage," he said. "There'll be a hammer and chisel in there."

And so, based solely on a tale told by a passing traveller, one whose very identity was in question, and bolstered by a hunch he could not ignore, my dad went to get that ancient tool box, possibly once used by Jan Piper, and subsequently smashed off the lock and threw back the lid.

A waft of camphor flew out. We both reeled back and then stared in. Lying on the top, on slats that lifted off, were several silk kimonos of red, green and blue, along with oriental fans and reams of silk – relics of a life brought back from the other side of the world, carried back to these shores a hundred years ago or more.

My mother's voice sounded as if it came from the end of a long drainpipe. Perhaps her stories of smuggling and looting from passing ships was right, she said, and one of the sailor's belongings had ended up here?

We never found out where it had come from. But buried beneath reams of fine cloth, silver tobacco and snuff tins, bundles of letters and a variety of aged hand-drawn maps, were hundreds upon hundreds of medical notes, all scripted on yellowed parchment in careful, looped italics. Any satisfaction in being right was grim. There was one for every patient, signs and symptoms, every drug ever administered, details of format and dose, all signed and dated by Doctor Tristan Bray.

Dad sat back on his heels.

"My God, he must have wanted them found!"

My mother glared at him.

"One day, long after he'd fled? Think about it! No one before us knew to look, no one whose interests it was in, anyway. Yet he left his records here. It's almost as if it was meant for us to–"

"It still isn't in anyone's interests, Jimmy."

Unless you were thoroughly haunted to the core of your soul. Or you had a moral compass... Or both...

Either way, Dad set about finding what he wanted, and he got it. The doctor, it seemed, had been every bit as professionally meticulous as him, with an analytical, logical mind that functioned with order and attention to detail.

It took time. He worked long into the night at the bureau downstairs, sectioning the relevant notes into bundles to take home. I remember eating toast by the fire in the lounge, watching him. No one told me to go to bed. It was the strangest night, and the one I think when everything changed for him as a human being, as a soul.

Once we got back to London, he made his own notes from both Tamara and Jowen's records, translating what was largely Latin script, abbreviated as is customary, the details of which he didn't share with me until around a decade later. After I'd become a nurse and might understand without being too badly affected.

They hadn't been what he'd expected. Not at all. And they threw a whole new light on the story.

***

CHAPTER TWENTY-TWO

The following is James Quiller's summary, which he passed to me having deciphered the handwritten script by Dr Tristan Bray, not wishing to carry them further with him on life's journey. The originals were lodged with Lovelyn and Waterford in Gulston, prior to probate.

Tamara Bray
Gorse Bank House, Hunters Combe, Devon

1872, January 2nd
Complains of fatigue, insomnia, loss of weight, headaches
Presents with a pallid complexion, bruised beneath the eyes, agitated, hysteria
⊠ *Laudanum, 10 drops nocté*

1872, February 14th
Physical symptoms – extreme fatigue, shivering and perspiring, excessively pale, somewhat breathless.
⊠ *Laudanum, 10 drops nocté*

March, 21st
Presentation, extreme fatigue, weakness, nose bleeds, breathless, chilled and pale. Myeloid Leukaemia suspected. Patient refuses to travel for a second opinion, preferring to

reside in the comfort of her own home. It is also preferred to not discuss the diagnosis with others in order to relieve them from distress

In addition, complains of itching, has taken to washing and scratching her skin at night, a condition of agitation and hysteria.

Nurse Peller referred to for soothing poultices

⊠ Laudanum 20 drops prn.

For the infant, Christopher, age 18 months, Royal Infants Preservative, Godfrey's Cordial, prn

April 7th

Complaints of nausea and cessation of monthly courses. Physical examination reveals a most unexpected pregnancy at approximately two and a half months.

Fragile physically, pale, listless, breathless and shivery, bruised eyes, exhaustion due to insomnia. In addition, olfactory delusions of sweet smoke in the house, and that her food tastes bitter, altered taste perceptions.

Referred to Nurse Peller for poultices to the skin, which is scratched and bleeding.

Repeat prescription for Laudanum, to be used prn for headaches, to provide rest and sleep, and to reduce excitable, restless behaviours.

Godfrey's Cordial for the child, Christopher, nocte and prn

July 2nd

Tamara has failed to gain weight in the second trimester, instead listless, pale, perspiring, breathless and shivery, confirming diagnosis of advanced myeloid leukaemia. It is to be hoped the pregnancy will progress full term despite the

patient's much weakened condition. Confidentiality requested in order not to distress relations
Itching skin and scratching, restless and agitated. Poultices to ease the distress.
Confinement advised.
⊠ *Laudanum 20 drops prn*

September 18th, 1872
3am Premature labour pains begin at an est. seven months, two weeks.
Rigid cervix, minimal dilation.
Nurse Peller in assistance
Tender swollen abdomen, bleeding excessive.
Tartar emetic administered, opium for pain relief.
Cervix smeared with extract of belladonna.
Fluids with honey administered by the nurse refused due to taste perception
Opium prn

An hour later the patient sleeps.

September 19th
4am Intense pain recurs
Cervix remains a rigid and bony ring
Tachycardia, incoherent ranting, confused and agitated, alternating with euphoria. Elevated blood pressure, skin red and hot. Thirst extreme. Fluids administered with a little honey, by Nurse Peller overnight.

1pm
Labour pains extreme. Opium for pain relief.

Aconite 20 drops to assist opening the cervix with a hope of saving the child, and treating the shock. Fluids with honey administered, further pain relief given.

September 21st
1am
Delivery of a premature child by Nurse Peller.
Patient deceased due to excessive blood loss

***

Jowen Trewhella
Trewhella Farm, Hunters Combe

9th October, 1872
Called to attend Jowen Trewhella, residing at Trewhella Farm, on the evening of October 9th following an accident at Withyarm Railway at 2pm. On arrival, clear symptoms of shock, skin ashen to grey in pallor, minimal and incoherent verbal response. Tachycardia, low diastolic pressure, commensurate with substantial blood loss and a severe wound to the right thigh.

⊠ *opium for immediate pain relief. A poultice of aconite applied to the wound, and fluids with honey administered by Nurse Peller, who stayed with the patient until he slept.*

10th October

Called 5.30am. Deceased. Cause of death, shock following grave bodily trauma

***

CHAPTER TWENTY-THREE

On their own, the notes meant little, as had the bundle of bones buried in the garden. But my dad was a chemist, who'd learned his profession in the post-war years when many nineteenth century physicians still practised, and whose copious notes remained in his possession. And on reading Dr Bray's records, his heart nearly short-circuited into fibrillation. They were not, as I said, what he expected.

There's an uncanny similarity, he explained, between the symptoms of myeloid leukaemia and laudanum poisoning. The two are almost identical. Except for one thing. By the time we sat down and discussed it, thrashing out our interpretations of what had most likely happened, I'd qualified as an SRN at the London Royal, and Dad lived alone above Quiller's Pharmacy on the corner of Camden High Street. It would have been 1973, the day sealed in my memory by a Stylistics song coming from a car radio outside, 'Betcha by golly, wow…' The day was warm, cherry blossoms dropping confetti on the pavement.

"How likely do you think it is, Enys, that Tamara never consulted her husband, at all? Never went to him as a patient?"

That hadn't actually occurred to me. I shook my head, puzzled.

"I don't mean by the time she was in labour, but before then. That the medical notes he wrote were left purposefully, almost with hubris, as a reputable and seemingly honest account of events should anyone be informed enough to question matters years down the line? Showing, perhaps, that he'd had nothing to hide, and was above reproach should that line of query even begin?"

I nodded. "Okay."

"I think they're a total fabrication, the whole lot. She never saw him for anything, had nothing to do with him, but he very shrewdly left a dead trail. So, should any member of her family for example, who'd noted how pale, breathless and thin Tamara was prior to death, suspect opium poisoning, it would be instantly quashed. Aha, so it was because she'd had myeloid leukaemia all along, a condition she wanted to keep from others in order to protect them from distress, even refusing a second diagnosis, preferring to stay at home. All bases covered. He even told the funeral congregation up front."

"Yes, I see."

"And medical notes are usually hurried, a pen grabbed here and there. Yet these for Tamara, and also for Jowen, are all in the same ink, in careful, methodical handwriting, as if they were written all in one go. The rest of his notes, for other patients, are more varied - some smudged, many illegible. Yet these are not illegible. They're absolutely clear."

"A re-written history?" I saw that perspective at once. "So, he knew his beautiful, wealthy wife didn't love him and never would. He'd been cuckolded, everyone was talking about it, and Tamara couldn't hide the fact, either – the boy Christopher was Jowen's double. Bray didn't own the house, it was hers, hadn't fathered either of the children, probably never got near her–"

My dad nodded.

"It's all theory, though. How could it be proven he poisoned her with laudanum?"

"Can't be done," he said. "Almost impossible and certainly in retrospect. Because he was quite clever."

"How so?"

"Look up the meaning of 'pharmacy'," he said. "There's often a razor's edge between a beneficial and a lethal dose, the difference between effective and toxic miniscule. Then look carefully at what he does in those notes. He prescribes a frequently used opium syrup, which is quite above reproach, but the side effects are respiratory depression, tiredness, weight loss, pale, luminescent skin and decreased appetite. All of that mimics the symptoms of leukaemia. The stuff's addictive, the more used the more needed, thus the greater the toxicity. A snowball effect. But he keeps the excess dosage hidden by prescribing it prn, in other words, as needed, hiding nothing. It's likely she would have taken some quite voluntarily at night, as many did, but with more, perhaps, added to food and drink without her knowledge. He states she had altered taste perceptions. Could that be in case she'd mentioned it to others? She also had itching skin, another sign of laudanum poisoning, but again he volunteers that information, not hiding it, explaining it as 'hysteria'."

"Hidden in plain sight, heading off objections before they're made?"

"Exactly. Answers for everything. But what's the one give-away sign of opium poisoning?"

"Pin-point pupils."

"So, what does a criminal mind do?"

"Disguise it."

Dad nodded. "I believe that long before the night of the guldize, he'd already started his revenge, slowly poisoning her body and mind, torturing a beautiful woman with the loss of her looks, and ultimately her power. Her golden glow soon faded to a pasty-grey sheen, her skin began to itch, she lost ever more sleep and weight, and the bewitching green eyes were far less attractive when dull and weary, with pinpoint pupils. All so conveniently explained away, and then expertly disguised at the last dying moments with a drug that would counteract the only thing giving it away."

"But there's no mention of… Oh, there is!"

"Yes. He mentions extract of belladonna applied to the cervix, which would have been proper at the time. Consider how much, though, may have been used? We don't know. In all the other patients' notes he records format and dosages precisely, except in Tamara and Jowen's case. But he does record it as used, and that would cover him nicely, should anyone ever enquire. Also, what about the honey water administered by Nurse Peller, something else that made perfect sense? It can be a lifesaver, yet Tamara initially refused it, due to 'taste perceptions', something referred to many months before, too, thus substantiating the claim at such a late stage. But what has a bitter taste? "

"Belladonna?"

"Absolutely it does – atropine."

"Which dilates the pupils at death, so if anyone saw the body and noticed–"

"Then they couldn't say it was laudanum poisoning, could they? It was well-known by then; a lot of people knew about the signs."

"But she drank it eventually, the honey water?"

"Think, Enys. What's a side effect of atropine?"

"Um, parasympathetic nervous system... um, dry mouth, racing heart, hot skin, hot as a hare..."

"Thirsty, then?"

"Yes."

"And probably very confused. With too much atropine, the vision can become blurred, the heart rate escalates, blood pressure's increasing, and there would be a hallucinatory effect similar to LSD. It's all in the dose, which is not recorded on these notes."

"You'd have to be very suspicious, to compare these notes with those of others and see how meticulous he normally was, but I suppose 'prn' covered him. Was it a legal requirement back then to record every dose, and what about the poultices?"

"It wasn't regulated as it is now, so the man doesn't even have to lie – his treatment protocol would easily have stood up in the court of the day and he knew it, although I'm pretty sure he was confident it would never come to that. To compound matters, aconite was also used – commonly known as wolfsbane or monkshood – a substance that would have been nigh impossible to detect after death, and again was routinely administered for all sorts of reasons, such as bladder pain, even symptoms as vague as fear and shock. But as always, it's the dose: too much and it would have rendered the woman numb in the face, blind, caused violent vomiting, and a feeling of impending dread. She would have had a horrible death, Enys. Debilitating, frightening and painful."

I was glad then, that he'd waited until I was at least

partially inured to sickness and death. I'd held swilling vomit bowls, drained noxious fluids from the diseased, held the hands of the dying, laid out corpses…

We sat in silence for a while.

"And Jowen?" I asked eventually. "What's your theory there? What he was given was natural enough and there wasn't much gone from the opium bottle, either?"

"Sugared water?"

"Oh God, yes."

"Think about the possibilities. He wouldn't have been in the least suspicious of Nancy Peller giving him honey water, would he? But what if it contained belladonna? A few sips and he'd be thirsty, his mouth sawdust-dry. By then he'd be away with the fairies too, on what was likely a large dose of opium from the doctor's black bag; and spying the water in the middle of the night, he'd have downed the lot in one go, I should imagine. That's one theory. Then there's the aconite poultice. Hidden in plain sight, again. Remember, there's a razor's edge between benefit and risk? A surprisingly tiny amount is fatal. If enough was used, he'd have died shortly after Nancy Peller left, with painful convulsions, nausea and vomiting, numbness to the face, then legs and arms, followed by a rapid heartrate and, possibly like Tamara, a feeling of dread. He, too, would have died in shock, horror and extreme pain."

"And quickly."

"Not before they'd both suffered a great deal. Minutes would have felt like hours. Tamara's was drawn out over several days, along with that of her unborn child."

The true gravitas, the evil of what the pair had done, began then to sink in.

"Such hatred. So well planned and executed."

"And we don't know what Nancy Peller's dressings and cordials contained. She could have been poisoning Tamara for quite a while."

"The notes mention sweet smoke in the house?"

"I don't know about that one, or why he'd record it, but I remember Silas Finn referring to Nancy Peller's walks in the woods, that she knew her henbane from her hemlock. Smoking henbane seeds almost certainly cause hallucinations."

"Oh God, poor Tamara."

"Yes, and she no doubt did it while Tamara was unconscious from laudanum. Anyway, that's why I think Bray was able to keep his counsel at the guldize, why he seemed to be the model of decorum and composure."

"Because they were already dealing with her..."

We sat in silence again. A group of people were laughing in the street below, and there was a waft of beer and fried food on the air.

They...

I began to ponder then. Nancy Peller had been present at every death.

"Silas Finn, Dad? He wasn't real, was he? I saw, you know? I saw him vanish into thin air. And I saw the ghost of Tamara too, you know I did. How else could I have described a woman frantically washing and scrubbing herself raw? I told you before he did."

"I don't want to think about that kind of thing, Enys," he said. "But I said I'd give you the notes when I thought you were ready and I've kept my promise. I believe I was right and Dr Bray did murder his wife and her child. Possibly her lover, too. And for the same reason as so many other atrocities, it was done out of jealousy and rage."

The fallout from the Christmas of 1962 had been devastating. Dad hadn't let it rest. There were Tristan Bray's notes, the bones found in the garden, and the physical attributes of those who came after, namely my mother and Ivy Trove – almost, it could be said, bringing to life the story Silas Finn had told, proving it, making it fit. Without Silas, none of that would have occurred, yet he didn't want to 'think about that kind of thing.'

And who had gained?

Certainly not the restless spirit in Gorse Bank House, but I'll come to that in a moment.

Victor Hamlyn had contested my mother's inheritance. The facts as known were presented at probate, and ultimately enough doubt was cast over the legitimacy of Mary Rose's line, as to call into question the validity of the Will, not least the birth register itself, which sealed my mother's fate. A modest sum was settled on her as a gesture of goodwill, but if Tamara had no legitimate descendants the house must revert to the Hamlyn Estate. They'd hired expensive lawyers and further contesting of the 'generous offer' would likely have eradicated any benefit. Thus, my mother conceded defeat and agreed. It wasn't the hundreds of thousands that would have set her free and bought a spacious house with a private garden, but it helped ease some of the financial worry after she and my dad broke up.

He loved my mum; I know he did. But he'd had to do the right thing, he said, couldn't have lived with himself if he hadn't. Mum chose a different perspective, and blamed him one hundred percent. It was all his fault. He'd put superstitious nonsense before his marriage and his family, and worst of all, sided with Ivy Trove. What good had come of that, she asked him? The wealthy got another house, and now she and Dad lived in flats, working all the hours. Well done, Jimmy. Bravo! So well done!

Dad was never the same after that. He went into himself somehow, no longer bounding out from the backroom of the pharmacy through the ribbon curtain, clutching a little packet of powder, peering over his spectacles to carefully read out the dosing instructions. Instead, he delegated most of the shop floor work to an assistant and spent much of his time upstairs, alone in his flat.

I don't believe for one minute that he didn't think about Silas Finn. I don't think he thought about much else.

To be perfectly honest, I was relieved the day he retired and sold up, bought a place on the Sussex coast, went walking every day with a dog, and met a woman he liked. For what it's worth, I think Victor Hamlyn would have contested anyway, based solely on the birth certificate, and all my dad did was make it that bit easier for him. What concerned me far more, was his refusal to address the supernatural aspect of what happened, at least not to me, but I wish he had because it might have explained why he'd felt so compelled to do what he did, and could have helped him emerge sooner from what was obviously, a pit of guilt.

I had my own pit of guilt, too. If only I hadn't demanded a story not a song, if only I hadn't wanted to please Beatrice, hadn't taken her to the apple tree and found the grave, if only I hadn't wanted so desperately to be liked, to belong, if only…

But I was ten. Lonely. Adrift. Scared. And I'd not only seen Tamara's ghost, but felt her presence and been the recipient of immense love. I'd also heard Silas Finn's story, then witnessed him vanish into the night air. And been every bit as swept up in the quest for truth as my dad had. If he would only concede there were unseen elements at work, I reasoned, then he wouldn't take the whole burden on himself. Maybe he'd understand some things are bigger, that it wasn't about a house, or even us, but about justice, conscience and honour within ourselves. But he would not discuss it, arguably the driving force that had shattered his life. Maybe the whole concept of the unseen was too disturbing, having the potential to unhinge a sane and rational man?

Well, I couldn't push anyone to do that, it's a soul decision, and besides, I was beginning to realise the baton had been passed to me. Maybe it was my turn? Because those dreams of Tamara were recurring more and more frequently and they weren't the nice ones, those had long gone. Once or twice I saw her face staring back at me in the mirror instead of my own, just for a second, enough to severely shock and unnerve. And sometimes, in the low ebb of my spirits in the hours before dawn, I'd jump-start awake, sure I'd heard a lock click open, or water splashing. Lying motionless, there would be no choice but to surrender to the memories of that ice-cold room and the gleam of the mirror in the corner, as my skin began to itch, a sweet, sickly smell of violets cloyed the air, and the sound of humming echoed around the walls…

Are you going to Scarborough fair…

Oh, we'd found out, or thought we had, what had happened in the house, felt we had laid the past to rest and righted the wrong. But all we'd done, all we'd lost and sacrificed, had actually made not one jot of difference to the unrest. In actual fact, it became worse. A lot worse. To the point where no one could live in the house at all.

And so, when I got the chance, I decided to find out directly – yes, to confront the restless spirit of Tamara Hamlyn myself. I don't know what drove me to do it. A curiosity to tear down the veil between worlds, to make sense of the face in the mirror, the one now in the back of my head, and the sweetly humming melody of increasingly lucid dreams. Or to solve the enigma of Silas Finn?

I only know I was haunted day and night. It needled me, it bugged me. And like my dad, I was hellbent on finding out why.

***

CHAPTER TWENTY-FOUR

Silas Finn had, for all those years, been at the root of the disquiet none of us discussed. Even Beatrice and I didn't talk about him and we talked a lot. The maths wasn't difficult – if he'd been twelve when Mary Rose was born, he'd have been a hundred and two that Christmas!

Be enough to make a restless spirit very angry indeed, I'd say. You'd haunt the place, wouldn't you? Could be the lady won't rest until the truth be found and the wrong be righted.

And inspired by his story, we'd acted on his words – wrongs had been outed that had shattered our family to the four winds, ruined lives, broken us – yet Tamara Hamlyn's spirit was allegedly angrier and more restless than ever! So who was Silas Finn? And what had been the purpose of his visit, if not to incite what we'd already done?

The only one I could really thrash things out with was Beatrice. We'd loosely kept in touch as teenagers, dutifully exchanging letters and cards, but it wasn't until we spoke on the phone in our early twenties, shortly after my dad showed me his notes, that I found out about the house.

In the mid-Sixties, Victor Hamlyn transferred Gorse Bank House to a young member of the family, who'd subsequently had it refurbished into the kind of home I'd always imagined it could be. Beatrice said there'd been workmen there for months – painters and decorators, plumbers for a new bathroom, electricians and so on. She'd flirted with them all, got to see the inside, and described deep pile carpets as was the fashion of the day, a coffee-coloured bathroom suite and a fitted kitchen. But within weeks of moving in, the couple fled. Just packed their bags, she said, and went back 'up along'. Never saw or heard from them again.

After that, for years it passed from one relation to another, none of them staying more than a few weeks, leaving it for the most part standing empty. Beatrice had done her best to find out why, unable to glean more than just, 'they couldn't settle'. Eventually though, through various cleaners who'd told others in the village, it transpired people had found the house depressing, caught shadows skittering across mirrors, dimming the stairwell, or they'd sensed something behind them when no one was there. They'd had nightmares, one door would constantly drift open, and children woke screaming. And then there was the way the whole house rattled and creaked even on a calm day, curtains billowed despite the absence of a breeze, fuses and light bulbs blew, fires wouldn't start, and a strangely sweet smoke sometimes filled the air.

Many years passed before, in the late Seventies, it was decided to rent the place out instead of leaving it empty; and initially many locals were grateful for the extra income derived from regular laundry, gardening and housework. But after a very short time it seemed the family's secrets could be kept no more, and rumours were rife in the village as a new generation spoke openly in The Tailor's Rest about the haunting of Gorse Bank House. Everyone, it seemed, now knew.

One of the cleaners, Della, had witnessed it herself. She'd been vacuuming the landing one day, when she'd heard a distinct click, looked up, and actually saw, with her own eyes, the middle bedroom door swing open. She described the atmosphere as crackling, static, as if time had stopped. But, with her heart pounding hard, she'd convinced herself it had been caused by a draught, that all the stories were made-up nonsense, largely because she didn't want them to be true and badly needed the job, and as such had gone to shut the door. But just as she grabbed the handle, she noticed a shadowy figure sitting on the window sill. And at that precise moment the whole room dimmed, and a freezing breeze blew around her shoulders. Terrified, she tore downstairs, straight out of the front door and all the way back to the village, convinced some horrible, creepy, shadowy thing was on her back. Her hair crawled with the feeling of it. She'd never go in there again. Not ever and not for any amount of money. It wasn't ghosts that scared her, she said – 'seen them afore' – but the feeling of huge menace, as if she'd be engulfed by a darkness it would be impossible to escape. No, she'd not be going in there again, would rather starve.

Beatrice told me all this during one of our long phone calls. Although she'd played the part all those years ago of a mischief-making teen with superior knowledge, the reality was she'd largely been alone with her confusion and fears; and although I'd assumed she and her mother were thick as thieves, that had been an assumption, too. Bea had garnered the bits she knew from eavesdropping, just as I had. There was a lot Ivy wouldn't discuss and as such, we both had a lot of questions that were never answered, which was why we picked at each other for scraps. One thing puzzling us both was why my mother had been adopted by the Trewhellas at the outset, brought up as one of their own, only to be so unceremoniously dumped later. Bea thought a sum of money was involved, that with no natural descendants, after Mary's death the house would have quietly and without objection, reverted to the Hamlyn family, as the contract specified when it was given to Tamara. No one, she said, had expected Mary to go to an outside solicitor, renege on the deal, and leave it to Josie with an explanatory, signed and witnessed letter. That had been a mighty blow. But she was only guessing.

I don't think Ivy wanted to tell Beatrice too much, but knowing Bea as I do, and how she can't keep anything inside no matter how big the secret, Ivy was probably very wise. I had a notion Mary knew her line had no legitimate right to the house, even if she didn't know about Enys or any murderous acts, and had perhaps hoped that by paying the Trewhellas to take Josie, a door would be closed. Bea thought the Hamlyns paid. The upshot, though, was that we never found out.

"My mother wouldn't have hurt your mum by saying that to her, anyway," Bea said. "That she'd been basically, sold."

"She did hurt her, though. She was really cruel to her at your grandmother's funeral."

Bea conceded. "Probably she was beside herself with grief. Left on her own with a farm at that age, and your mum was horrible to her growing up – they fought a lot. I'm not making excuses, Enys Quiller."

"I know."

The main thing that kept Bea and I on the hotwire to each other though, long after she married and had children, was the haunted house and how it affected one tenant after the next. I'd confided in her about the apparition in the mirror, the strange lucid dreams, including the jack-in-the-box and the shawl found later. How could I have known any of that before hearing Silas Finn's story, and before my dad emptied those boxes? And then there'd been the obvious evidence we'd dug up ourselves. The story fitted. But we'd overlooked some key detail. There had to be more to it than we thought, a reason for the continuing and escalating disquiet. We were, as said, uncommonly fascinated. But we were also missing something, and when I found out what that was, it was almost too late. Because it had been there all along… waiting patiently, and then less patiently, for me to notice.

But before I got to that stage, before it was facilitated, you might say, there'd been another phone call with Bea. It was the early Eighties. I'd taken the call on the stairs outside my flat and Spandau Ballet was playing in the flat downstairs, 'I know that… much is… true…' Bea had been talking about her daughter's first day at school, when we'd circled once more to the subject that bonded us. The house had gained such a reputation by then, that it couldn't even be rented – prospective tenants were asking the agents why it was such a good price, what had happened to the last occupants, and a few articles had been written about it being one of the most haunted houses in Britain.

Once again it stood empty.

I'd gripped the receiver as if it was a lifeline, hungry for ever more news. Unlike Bea, I wasn't happily married with children. Nor was I engrossed in a riveting career. You could say I was disturbed… distracted… tormented even. Had become a misfit, drifting in and out of jobs, not able to settle to anything.

After the Christmas of 1962, my mother had flat-out

refused to acknowledge the house's existence, never wanted Hunters Combe mentioned again, and most particularly wouldn't hear the name, 'Ivy Trove'. I'm going to say that when she realised my part in the disinterment, she did her duty by me and nothing more. At eighteen, I was to leave as soon as possible, and after a few years she remarried – to an ex-military man, very proper, very gentlemanly, but not, absolutely not, up for a discussion on a haunted house. And so Bea was my only link. Sometimes that was tenuous, and sometimes I felt I should let her go, too. But then she'd come and find me. And the conclusion we came to was this: Tamara was not at peace and not satisfied with anything that had been done. So, what had we got wrong? And why had Silas Finn, whoever he was, led us in the wrong direction?

"Different ways of taking folks to the pisky bog," Bea once said. "Different piper. Different tune. Same bog."

That stuck with me.

Anyway, the last lot of tenants had abandoned the house in two days.

And before they left, Beatrice said, they dropped into The Tailor's Rest, where they duly told their story. Their dog, a springer spaniel, had refused point blank to venture any further into the house than the hall. Whining, he'd slunk back to the porch and stayed there. The woman, an aromatherapist, who'd wanted to run her business from home, had walked in and immediately seen, on the periphery of her vision, a shadow form flit across the stairwell. Later that afternoon, she noticed another in the reflection of a mirror upstairs, but not wanting to annoy her husband or sound fanciful, she didn't say anything. But that night she awoke to the sound of a cot creaking. Try as she might, she could not get back to sleep, the house, on a perfectly calm tranquil night, besieged by rattling blinds and door handles, a strong smell of sweet smoke, and the frequent ping of the telephone downstairs. Next morning, she noticed again a shadow cross the hall as she came downstairs, and the lights periodically dimmed and flickered. Quiet at breakfast, her husband asked what was wrong, and expressed concern about the dog, who wouldn't come into the house.

"You don't think it's really haunted, do you?" he joked.

Uneasy, the woman pretended all was well, replying glibly it was just a new house, that the dog would settle in soon. At that point, she was completely unaware that her husband had also lain awake, watching shadows scoot across the dressing table mirror, listening to a door rattle somewhere, as if someone wanted to get out but couldn't. Neither, however, had told the other. The country house was all they'd wanted, had dreamed of. And so that night they went to bed, tired, reading by lamplight until they drifted off. When, at around one in the morning they started awake at the same time. They couldn't say why. One said they'd heard whispering, the other splashing water. But the air was freezing and they each lay with breath held, when they saw at the same time a woman glaring out of the mirror over the mantelpiece, in their own words, 'a furious-looking, deathly white creature with tar-black eyes.'

They both leapt out of bed and put all the lights on.

And even as they were loading up the boot next morning, there'd been a feeling of being watched from the house, the observer melting away the moment they looked up.

"Bloody hell!"

"I know," said Beatrice.

"The mirror... would it be a new one or the oval one that used to be in my bedroom?"

"I don't know. I can try and find out. Anyway, Victor Hamlyn said they're going to use it as a holiday home now, instead. S'ppose they're hoping grockels will last at least a week."

"Does Victor still visit your mum, then?"

"Oh God, yes! At least my dad's not around to witness it anymore, I s'ppose."

"It must have been awful for him."

"Yeah, well. At least he never knew about the others. I don't think so, anyway."

Others?

"Anyway, Victor's having a swimming pool put in," Bea was saying. "And the barns are going to be converted into garages and a games room. I think they're hoping to bring some business to the village, maybe hire out some of the old cottages and convert the old mill to a restaurant. I might start running pony treks or something..."

But I was no longer listening. Had almost missed it... A holiday let! Of course!

I had to go there, to the house. I had to confront Tamara's spirit. It had to be me. Somehow it had to be me and could not be anyone else. She was calling to me, you see? In dreams. I had felt that slice of ice-coldness again, the shiver of silk against my cheek, as if she'd found me. Needed me.

Enys... Enys...

And so now I could go. A holiday let. Perfect.

***

CHAPTER TWENTY-FIVE

There was time to prepare. According to Beatrice, it would take at least a year for the house to be upgraded.

Good, I thought, because I wanted to research spiritualism.

By then, and I accept this now, the whole thing had become an obsession. I'd single-mindedly convinced myself I had to help Tamara, that we'd overlooked something important. Sometimes I could feel her rage, once or twice fingers pressed into my windpipe at night, a feeling of suffocation and panic. Silas Finn had entrusted us with a sacred message, and for one reason or another, we'd each failed.

Mediums spoke to the dead, didn't they? Well, I reasoned, if Tamara had appeared to me after death, in dreams, then maybe I could communicate with her as an adult, put aside my fears of the unknown, and find out what it was that would bring her peace.

In retrospect, I'm aware now that my motives had never been as altruistic as I thought. But my veil of delusion was not one I even knew existed at the time, that being the nature of both veils and delusions. The removal of both can shock the mind, if done too quickly, thus the process was slow and, as Bea might say, 'dreadful pained'. I only know I was driven to do what I did and had to go through it. My own life was passing in a blur, I was barely conscious in the present moment, suspended as I was between the past and some vague notion of a future where everything became clear. And I don't even think it was Tamara who was the core of the obsession. Rather, it was Silas Finn.

Thing was, I could almost convince myself Tamara was a figment of my imagination, a dream, a nightmare even. But with Silas Finn I couldn't. He'd appeared to all three of us, as real as any other mortal being. And then all three had either seen or heard him walk down the hallway to the porch and take his leave. Yet there'd been no footprints. That single moment of shock had fractured the fabric of our fragile realities, after which nothing had been the same again. While my mother had refused to acknowledge the enormity, however, and my dad had perhaps gone as far as he could, for me the journey had barely begun. Nothing was as it seemed, there were others around us, residing in parallel realms. Occasionally, one or other of us saw their shadows, their imprints, but could they see us? Oh, how I wanted to know!

I'd long become restless as a nurse, frustrated with the all-consuming workload of daily tasks and unsociable hours. The only part I truly enjoyed, hand on heart, was talking to patients, hearing their stories, being the one they unburdened themselves to, especially during the early hours. They'd confide then; secret, buried things, recount chance encounters that had saved their life or dramatically altered it, something inexplicable they had to get off their chest. Emotionally, I seized these revelations, marvelling at the invisible connection with others I felt sure existed. And then came the near-death experience, my own chance encounter, one that dramatically altered the course of my life when the time came, the significance of which I almost missed.

It happened when I was working nights in Casualty. A woman in her early forties technically died for several minutes following a car accident, had flatlined, and while the team set to work with defibrillators, there was a very specific exchange of words between the medics. A few hours later, I was sitting with her while we waited for a porter to take her to the ward, when all of a sudden she opened her eyes and related exactly what they'd said.

"I was out of my body," she told me. "Standing against the far wall by a sink, watching the body of a woman on the table jump violently from electric shocks. I heard them shout, 'Stand back!' and then one of them asked if I was married or not. Had anyone phoned the husband? Someone else was saying they hadn't had a break yet, and another one asked if anyone had seen the registrar, Malcolm Garland. Then I watched them inject something into my chest and the one with black curly hair shook his head and said, 'She's gone.'"

She was spot on.

She'd not only heard them but described everyone in the room and beyond. She told me all the stress and pain left her instantly, how she'd been able to watch with curiosity, her whole being full of overwhelming calm and peace. Her perceptions then increased exponentially, and there was a feeling of becoming all-seeing, all-knowing, experiencing an omnipresence. She'd wanted to know her own family was all right, and immediately found herself next to her twenty-year old daughter, who was at that moment walking through the park with her boyfriend. There was love between them, she said, and she knew she'd be okay. Then her husband. She saw him taking a phone call, saw him nodding, and knew he was being told about the accident. After which he'd put the phone down, snapped open a can of beer, and slumped onto the sofa to watch a football match. He'd been smiling.

About to sympathise, I was cut short when she added, "What a blessing to find out now! I won't be wasting the rest of my life on him, trying to please him, letting him guilt, rebuke and shame me. I know what that may sound like, but it's just as if all the pain I know I would have felt, has already been wiped clean. I've been set free. Deep inside I knew already, you see? Oh, there are a lot who'll say I didn't. But I did. I just didn't listen to myself, didn't trust myself, kept hanging on… because of fear… fear of what? I kept myself in the trap, don't you see? I gave all my power away. I don't even feel sad. I just woke up feeling totally different."

She had a look of awe on her face, almost rapture.

"I don't know if this makes any sense to you, but he's not the centre of my world at all. No one is. My life is actually about me. I'm supposed to learn about me!"

Shortly afterwards, I left the hospital and, living off savings and a part-time job in a nursing home, began to study the occult, or the unseen. There were thousands upon thousands of books, religious and scientific, ancient scripts, articles, tapes, personal testimonies and photographs. I even followed a spiritual medium around for a while. I discovered there were non-human entities, and that ghosts were energetic imprints, that it was all about energy and frequency, absorbing everything I could, while falling short of understanding the one vital connection I should have made.

Nevertheless, after an intense eighteen months, and starting to run low on funds, I felt I was ready to go back to Gorse Bank House.

There's a reason for everything, I told myself. And Silas Finn, whoever he was, had visited our family that night and told that particular story. Why? He'd pretty much spelled it out, yet what we'd done had not only made no difference whatsoever to Tamara's restless spirit, it had actually made matters worse for everyone involved. So why did she remain angry? Hadn't we unearthed the facts for her? Why did she linger? Surely she only damaged herself? All the other players were gone. So why did she remain in torment and what could be done?

Here was my theory, and where the astute will note I failed to make that all-important connection, but at the time I was excited, making my beliefs fit into the frame. My logic was this and it married my research with experience – that at the point of death, Tamara had been heavily drugged. She couldn't have known up until then that her husband had been slowly poisoning her, having become gradually more brain-addled and unwell, focusing solely on Jowen Trewhella coming for her and Christopher. And so instead of enlightenment as the soul passed from the body, had she in fact remained in a state of drugged confusion – influenced by hallucinatory substances that both blinded and affected the part of the brain producing a sense of doom? Her energy vibration would have been low, in a state of extreme terror. As such, perhaps she'd been unable to ascend, trapped instead in confusion, pain and fear?

As such, while Silas Finn's message was clear, had the reason behind her continued presence been either misconstrued or totally missed? The concept of ghosts lingering until a wrong was righted was a principle I finally began to question. Who inherited the house had been of little consequence, the burial of the baby in hallowed ground brought no relief, nor the exposure of Tristan and Nancy's actions. So what, then, would bring her peace?

So, this was why I took the decision I did. By then, I was convinced Tamara was still there, frozen in the crystallised moment she left her body, remaining locked in the same state of shock and disbelief. Still confused and terrified. She relived it day after day. Locked in the horror of it with no way out. Who was sleeping in her child's bed? Who was staring at her in the mirror? Nothing made sense to her.

I believed she was frightened and utterly lost. And I also believed it must be me who helped her. It had to be someone who knew every detail as far as possible, who could communicate and explain it all to her, one who cared deeply and was personally involved. I had felt that love, I had a connection, knew I could help her and was absolutely convinced of that. I even fancied I was Enys reincarnated, that I was her and she me. Silas Finn had told us the story, and only us, but my mother and father had walked away. It had to be me!

Enys... Enys...

So, under a different name, I booked a week's holiday at Gorse Bank House. It was mid-September, a date which coincided with the traditional guldize in the village, when Bea would be especially busy. By then, she was running a pony trekking business as well as the farm. I didn't tell her about my visit. I didn't tell anyone. Not until afterwards. I planned to be totally undisturbed.

The one who laid Tamara's ghost to rest. To be the

one.

This all be on your shoulders now, Enys Quiller.

Some things run deep.

***

Chapter Twenty-Six

Gorse Bank House, Hunters Combe, Devon

1987 and the house had changed almost beyond recognition. Painted white with pale blue window frames, it was double-glazed, the nearest barn now a slick car port, the once bleak driveway lined with mature rhododendrons, choisya, and laurels. Cedars and pines bordered the open fields, providing a wind shield that cocooned the garden, and on that late summer day as I approached the honeysuckle-covered porch, it seemed to shimmer in a haze of drowsy bees, toppling hollyhocks and scented roses. It was beautiful, far more so than I'd ever imagined, and its magic clutched at my heart.

Inside, the house was cool. Dust motes swirled and danced in a single golden ray as I opened the door, the air fragrant with beeswax, freshly cut flowers and a bowl of red apples. The original flagstones remained in the hall, but the walls were now painted white and there were gleaming floorboards throughout. The kitchen had a shiny blue Aga and, in the style of the Eighties, wall-to-wall oak cupboards. A conservatory had been added to a lounge furnished with several deeply comfortable-looking sofas, and where there'd been a flat expanse of lawn, there was now a covered swimming pool and a tennis court.

It had a stillness to it, an air of anticipation as if a play had yet to begin; and tentatively, determined not to be anxious, I went upstairs.

Although I'd seen the advertising brochure, and knew all six bedrooms had been opened up, it nevertheless came as a surprise when I saw it - whoever had made the decision to convert the middle room to a nursery, must either have been completely insensitive or woefully ignorant of its history. My heart lurched uncomfortably at the sight. Whatever must Tamara feel about this? That was my initial thought.

Everyone knew the story here. Everyone. How could they have done this?

The room was furnished with a small bed, a cot, a rocking horse, and a single white wardrobe with a matching chest of drawers. The curtains were lemon, the walls – the only ones in the house that were papered – patterned with teddy bears. A fluffy white sheepskin rug lay on the floor by the hearth, there was an oval mirror above the fireplace, and the window seat was now padded with fitted cushions. Made to sit on. To be comfortable on. Easy to reach for one of the fairy-tale books on the shelf, or perhaps to simply sit and gaze up at the moors, at the stone circle, and the lane… at whoever might come down it… while keeping an eye on the baby in the cot by the wall…The layout, in other words, almost exactly as it had been over a hundred years before.

I stood for a while, quashing the memory of my father on his knees the last time I saw it, emptying the chest, hair plastered to his forehead, hellbent on finding those notes.

The atmosphere, however, was calm, quite blissful, and I soon brought my breathing under control, letting the essence of the house settle around me, gradually becoming aware of the energies that had been and gone, of the layers peeling back, years of voices calling to each other, doors slamming and baths running; then the smell of wet plaster and paint, the sound of saws, hammering of nails, electric drills, drifting further and further back in time, to the long, silent years when only Mary had lived here. To when she'd sat on the window seat, seen by all who'd passed, staring out, as if she hadn't been living at all, as if she was simply waiting. And waiting. For what? For what, Mary?

And why did you let your granddaughter go? Then change your mind and make a different claim?

As the sun began to dip, I, too, went to sit on the window seat, captivated by the glory of the dying day. There really are no words to capture the miracle of creation and our ability to see such beauty. I felt my eyes sting with a lifetime of unshed tears. Dusk was a rose quartz sky imbued with violet, the gilt-edged bracken on the moors fiery in the majestic coppery light. The fall of evening shadows came in barely perceptible degrees, the wings of a heart-faced barn owl swooping past swift and low, lamps flicking on in cottages dotted along the hills. Until slowly, almost imperceptibly, the house sank into darkness.

Still I sat, waiting patiently, as I had once watched spiritual mediums wait.

Tamara. Would she come?

My voice, when I eventually spoke, sounded feeble and self-conscious, but I was alone and there was no one to care what I sounded like. No one to impress, prove anything to, or give out diplomas. This was simply me on my own. And my chance to face what had gnawed away at me all these years.

Banishing fears of the door to the landing slamming shut as it had for Duffy Piper, and tales of being engulfed by freezing darkness, I began instead to build up a visual image of white light around me, and I prayed then, asking for protection, knowing in my heart that it was given and in abundance.

My voice ricocheted around the room. "I'm here, Tamara. My name is Enys Quiller and I've come to set you free."

There wasn't a sound.

It was a tranquil evening, soft as velvet, a band of pale sky on the horizon. Perhaps, I was too early? Or did I need to think of her, to focus on her image?

Accordingly, I closed my eyes and did what I hadn't done in years, daring to picture Tamara as she'd appeared in my dreams, purposefully conjuring her face as she'd smiled down at me. I heard again the faint squeak of a cot, falling back into the role, gazing at her on the window seat across the room, deep azure sky behind. I fixated on the necklace of beads, on the crocheted shawl around her shoulders, on that hot, hot day…

"Tamara," I said. "I need to explain what I think happened to you when you passed. I understand your confusion, your shock, your frustration. But you're free now. It happened a century ago, and everyone else is long gone."

I sat there until the night air breathed its chill into my bones. And I told her the whole story, explaining how traumatised souls often didn't know they were dead, how drugs or heavy drink could obscure the conscious mind, how anger and fear could entrap. And then I told her my own story, I poured out my heart, even that I thought I could be Enys reincarnated, a theme I'd increasingly warmed to.

But there was no response. Absolutely nothing.

From the valley below, the jaunty strain of a fiddle carried on the night air; a party, the guldize… something for others not me… Tears prickled my eyes again.

A full moon had risen, floating over the moors, a luminescent balloon in an inky sky. And awareness filtered in then, that the empty silence hissing around me was akin to that of a tomb. It wasn't so much the lack of response, rather the lack of anything, an absence of life, the room an echoing, dank, underground chamber that smelled ever so faintly of rotting flower stems. My heart snagged on its pulse. And for the first time since I'd entered the house, unease prickled all over my back.

I stared out at the silvery thread of the lane.

I'd got this horribly wrong, hadn't I?

All at once, what I was doing felt flat, fake… risible even. And with that thought, there came a distinct sense of being laughed at, mocked, of muffled giggles and whispers behind unseen hands. All of a sudden I felt strangely threatened and jumped up.

I switched on all the lights and hurried downstairs. I was tired, hungry and getting cold. I'd feel better after a bite to eat, that was all. It was disappointment, an anti-climax, self-doubt, all those things.

The house was airy, light and clean, and had been totally transformed since the last time I'd been there, yet when I walked into the lounge with sandwich and coffee, for a moment I thought I saw the old bureau by the window; and an odour of mildew wafted on the air like decaying hymn books. Hesitating, I stood in the doorway. The impression then faded and I switched on the lamp and ate the sandwich. I'd have a bath, relax, try to communicate with Tamara again later, I decided. She'd always visited after I'd gone to sleep. Maybe that was it? Only, deep in the core of my soul, I knew it wasn't.

At eleven o'clock that night, I then went back to the room with the round window. The harvest moon, by that time, was overhead, bathing the moors and fields in its milky light. I had taken this long journey to help a trapped soul and, no matter my own fears and limitations, I would overcome them to help her. It felt, had always felt, like a mission. And so this time I went to the small bed by the wall, sat down and prayed, then began again the process of protection and surrounding myself in divine light before once more picturing her as I remembered. I was a child in a cot, she on the seat by the window.

"Tamara Hamlyn, are you here?"

I repeated the question several times, momentarily unnerved by a floorboard creaking on the landing. It was just expansion and contraction, I reassured myself, and it was crucial not to descend into fear.

Stop it, Enys! Stop it. Think of the love between you... Capture that feeling, concentrate on that!

I had seen love in her eyes. The woman had been full of love, for Christopher, for her unborn child, for Jowen. She could not be an angry creature full of hate, deliberately terrifying others. She was merely frightened and confused.

Enys... Enys...

I could reach her consciousness. Whatever state of fear

and frustration she was locked in, she could be freed if only she knew she was loved.

"Tamara, can you hear me? I can help you. I know what happened. You're trapped in shock and–"

A floorboard creaked directly in front of me, then loudly, a matter of feet away, just as if a grown man had walked into the room. My heart jack-hammered into my chest and then the room instantly shot to black. No warning. No degrees. Straight to freezing. Into my mind's eye came a horrific vision of myself tugging at the door, shut fast, unable to escape, wild-eyed, screaming, no one to hear…

Immediately I shut it down, forcing into my head a powerful wall of blinding white light instead, citing the Lord's Prayer and requesting divine protection, believing and knowing it was already done. I could and would do this. She was angry, confused, scared, and, hardly surprisingly, untrusting!

"I know you're here, Tamara. But you must understand you've left the body now, and that what hap–"

It was unmistakeable and shut me up instantly – a crepuscular rustle of a long silk dress, and a sigh of breath in the far recess of the room. Followed by a waft of air as if someone had just walked past.

She's going to materialise!

"Hello, Tamara!"

My heart was nearly in my mouth, so high had it jumped, but I pressed on, remembering how the spiritual medium I'd followed around had never once baulked. She'd hadn't been worried at all, sending spirits off to the light, passing messages back and forth.

Who was she really talking to?

I refused to listen to my own voice. No, this was just my own fear and must be conquered.

"You're constantly reliving your torment," I told her. "But you've passed over to Spirit now, Tamara, and so has everyone else from that time. You've left the body, and your child, Enys, has now received a proper burial, the wrongs have been brought into the light. We did everything we could..."

I stopped, thought then, but immediately dismissed the notion, that I'd heard a snicker of laughter, like someone had slapped a hand over their mouth to contain a burst of mirth.

"You are free," I persisted. "What keeps you here?"

Then came a sound I hadn't heard in over twenty years. There was a tug of alarm. Something was badly wrong. But again, I tamped it down. No fear. Be in control. Soon, as had happened with the spiritual medium I'd watched time and again, this tortured soul would be free and the house would be restored to peace.

Who was she really talking to?

I took a series of deep breaths, shutting the annoying voice up. "Tamara, you are free to return to perfect love and bliss, to continue your spiritual journey and evolve as a soul. This is only an experience, a brief–"

No, I hadn't been mistaken.

Splashing. Splashing water.

My eyes scanned the dark room, settling, to my horror, on the oval mirror above the fireplace. And just as if I was ten years old all over again, my mind almost blanked out as someone else's eyes then met mine in the pearlescent moonlit reflection.

It wasn't Tamara.

She would have had a horrible death, Enys. Debilitating, frightening and painful.

Oh God! I should have realised. What I'd missed!

It wasn't Tamara and it never had been.

In a flash it hit me, the crucial detail I'd failed to acknowledge: the woman who'd had the near-death experience, who'd also been given strong drugs, had said there was no emotion after leaving the body, only peace, understanding, and unconditional eternal love. But no emotion! So why had I thought Tamara, a woman consumed with love, driven by love, would be an exception?

And if this wasn't Tamara, then who was it? Not a trapped human soul but trapped energy? Shit! Of course! An energy that had grown and grown with each consecutive fearful tenant, one that had snowballed with all the entities now attracted to it. Negative entities that mimicked the deceased, that were brought in by…

Who did she really work with?

Holy crap! What was in here with me?

"I do not consent to dark or negative forces. I do not consent to the dark or the negative. I do not consent…"

In one moment of blind panic, one mighty heart thump, along came the sure-fire knowledge that what I was facing alone, with no one even knowing I was here, was demonic. A relentless hatred with no mercy, that few acknowledged as existing until it was too late, that latched onto the living having fooled and tricked its way in…. or … and here was the worst thought… being conjured by those who thought they could control it.

Once in, it was in.

But if a demon was controlled it ceased to be evil, did it

not? It became a slave, thus losing its power. What a risk for a demon, therefore, to consent to a summoning! But if it had, then once here, it must have the upper hand.

I was desperately trying to keep calm as all at once everything made sense, flying into my face with all the terror of a speeding freight train. Of course – those stones I'd found in the wall, the burning henbane seeds, the crocheted shawl, the beaded necklace, and…what about the mirror? I yanked it off the wall and stared at a sigil etched on the back.

All the research I'd done, yet when it was in my own face I'd so nearly missed it.

Nancy Peller!

Not a few herbs and poultices, but full-blown dark arts. Tamara's friend and nurse, Tristan's lover, Mary's mother… Everyone in this house had either died or gone mad! I was almost sick. She'd sent them all mad. Not only that but she'd tended to the dying, to new-borns, everyone thought she was wonderful, had invited her into their homes, accepted stitched and woven gifts…

So! What had she brought in?

Ee knew her henbane from her hemlock…

As all those thoughts began to crowd into my head – working with demonic entities, using words as spells, sewing intent into shawls and bracelets, marking areas with sigils on stones, trees, mirrors… it occurred to me maybe Tristan Bray had known, had left a hint to that effect buried in the notes acknowledging sweet smoke… Had he become aware of his own madness and fled to save himself? And what about Mary Rose? Had she known?

The cot in the corner began to swing and creak in the umbra of the shadow, and as I whirled round, the memory of my childhood dream resurfaced. Somehow that thing, whatever entity Nancy had brought into our world, had projected images, energetic echoes, into my dreams!

It happened fast after that. A heady, sickly scent of decay and violets filled the room, and an icy wind shivered into my back, along with a sensation of being towered over. Like a mouse in a field, it was as if the wings of an overhead buzzard had rapidly shadowed the ground and there was no escape. Dark shapes materialised from out of the walls before my eyes, a throng of them, from all sides, every angle. Coming for me! Horrified, I felt then, fingers pressing into my throat as they had in my nightmares, there was a roar in my ears and I braced myself for the door to slam shut. It was all I could do not to reconjure the image Duffy Piper had relayed of being engulfed. Only there was no Jan to come and find me. I was going to black out…

My strength, when it came though, flashed up so powerfully my whole body shook.

"In the name of our Father, the Father of all there is, has been and ever will be, I command you to return from whence you came and do not come back."

Failure was not an option.

"Return from whence you came and do not come back. Return from whence you came…"

It seemed to last for hours. At times it was almost impossible to draw breath, the stench of decay was suffocating, my throat felt constricted, and it was an effort to stay awake. I sat in a vision of blinding white light that took every ounce of mental strength to maintain, repeating my refusal to consent to the dark, allowing only love to flood my being, holding onto all the things for which to be grateful, determined not to be the woman screaming to get out of a locked room, adding to all the terror and fear in the world. Until finally, out of nowhere I recalled the words once heard in the early hours of the morning, from the lady who'd had the car accident, words I'd long since suppressed that were desperate to be heard:

It's actually about me. I'm supposed to learn about me.

And that's when everything switched in a heartbeat. Not only had this never been Tamara Hamlyn, it wasn't about her, either. She was long gone. It was about me. I was the one who was trapped in my own mind, stuck in a twenty-plus-year obsession, and those demons had fed off my fear of not belonging, of abandonment, of my mother drifting away, of the unknown, and tales of a mad old woman's ghost. I'd been sucked into the empty, howling abyss of fear, as inevitably as water swirls down a drain, and whatever entity had attached to me during the Christmas of 1962, had followed me home and stayed. What the hell had happened to my life?

This was my fear. All my own fear.

I stood up then. Walked over and switched the light on.

"Enough," I said out loud. "You don't exist to me."

There was an icy blast on my face but I walked through it. I think I was so shocked, so appalled, that I'd got to my mid-thirties and was living in near poverty, pouring through books on the dead instead of living my life to the full. I hadn't been out with anyone in years, had no family of my own, and a career covered in dust sheets. I wasn't angry, but the veil was torn down, I saw the trick, and the voltage was enough to resurrect a corpse.

Deluded, I'd been every bit as insane as all the others.

But no more. Not one more day!

The door opened straight away. I meant to collect my

things and drive to the coast, to let the bracing sea air heal my shattered psyche. But here's something that sits at odds with all I've said even now. And I swear on my own life I heard it.

As I walked out of that room I heard, "Enys! Enys! Thank you."

But that could have been of my own creation, too.

***

Epilogue

Present Day. September 21st, 2022

I'd never set foot in The Tailor's Rest until the day I finally met up with Beatrice for lunch. I was seventy, she seventy-two. She'd put on weight, a big woman by then, although I daresay my late mother would have been a lot less charitable in that regard. But for one who'd been so lithe, so slender of limb, she was certainly well-padded and it was quite a surprise. Happy though, joy bursting out of her, especially after the bottle of wine we sank.

"Good to see you didn't get the crooked spine, Enys Quiller," she said as we sat down.

I laughed. "You and the crooked spine stories!"

"Did your mother, you know… succumb?"

I shook my head. "Nothing you'd notice. Not the hunchback of Notre Dame you're imagining, anyway."

I'd never been able to speak about what happened at Gorse Bank House, largely because it was so intensely personal. With the appalling realisation I'd had a dark attachment, one that leeched off me and wanted to destroy me, I'd had a lot of inner work to do. I began to think that's what had happened to all of them in that house, including Nancy Peller, in the end. My shadow side had been the fear of abandonment, something that dogged me into adulthood, a feeling of not being loved. There was no point blaming anyone - they had their own issues to deal with - because in the end no one else could help me. It had to come from within. And that took some facing up to, a lot of work, and a long time.

I married quite late, at thirty-nine, didn't have children, but I did pursue a career that brought immense pleasure. I asked myself one day what I loved. What set my soul on fire? And the answer came shortly after, when I was searching the jobs section in the paper. Suddenly there it was. I'd always loved old stories, secret histories and magical tales, was curious and passionate about them, believing there was usually an element of truth, and nothing was to be dismissed as impossible. Who's to say? And there was a publisher advertising for editorial staff. Of course, I hadn't the qualifications. But I set about getting them, and took low-paid work in the meantime. After that, I worked in drama production, eventually writing scripts and bringing them to life. I've loved it. Every minute. And my husband's a sound engineer, although long since retired. If I could have another life, I'd go for costume design, anything that's creative and keeps ancient tales alive, for what brings joy and colour to our lives? The droll teller may say different ways of looking at things…

Well, after we'd had a catch-up, which took a few hours, the landlord let us stay all afternoon seeing as how he'd always had a soft spot for Bea. She winked.

"Had a lot of fun in my time, Enys Quiller."

"I can believe that."

But afterwards, in the quiet of the inn's empty tap room, I did tell her about it. She was the only person I'd ever confided in, the only one who wouldn't write me off as nuts. But when I finished, even she was pretty lost for words.

"Bloody hell. You went and did that on your own?"

"I had to. I was like a worker bee pulled back to the hive. It was on my mind all the time, Bea. I couldn't sleep without seeing that ghastly face in the mirror, couldn't shake the horror of those dreams, of the ghost lunging into my face, all bleeding arms and eyes black as flour weevils. I was never truly myself, either – I was depressed, trying constantly to please people but it never worked, I was tired all the time. It just never hit me, that's all, that I could stop it. That however this stuff works, and it does or dark arts wouldn't be rife to this day, I didn't have to submit to it."

"So you reckon whatever attached to you wanted you to go back there so the power of it could sort of… what… walk into you? Possess you?"

"There was more than one. The room was full of them like other people said, crowds of them surging towards me, the blackness was overpowering. I could hardly breathe."

Her eyes narrowed. "But it backfired. How?"

"Because I did enough homework to know it wasn't Tamara. That was the trick, see? It was never her. Nancy Peller brought those demonic entities in and they overcame her in the end, too. Made her drink herself to death."

"Took her soul?"

"I don't know. But yes, you're right, I think it was a possession attempt. They've to send you mad, isolate you, terrify you. It felt like a snuffing out of conscious life, of free will, that's the only way I can describe it."

"Do you believe that?"

"I don't not believe it. I think certain healers get their

healing powers from the dark, too. False light. Imprint signs on those who trust them. That's how it can be done, the dark working without consent. I think Nancy did that!"

"You've given me the creeps now. I had a massage last week from this woman in Gulston, and halfway through she was telling me she did the tarot."

"I'm sure you'll be fine."

"I'll have to get a few bits of fuckery out of my head now, though." She uncorked another bottle of wine. "You were clever, you know? Eventually."

"No, I was stupid. But I didn't know I was stupid. Bit like death really, when you're stupid – it's only others that suffer. We're here to learn, I suppose."

She laughed. "And what have you learnt, Enys Quiller?"

I shook my head. Some things were too deep, had taken too long to acknowledge and process. But there was one thing I could tell her. "That all of this is for us. We're always looking at others, discussing them, trying to help or judging them. When all the time it's us we're supposed to be improving. All these things that happen to us, that we complain about, and we're victims, right? People were mean? Or, were they lessons we're supposed to notice and if we don't, they'll get bigger and bigger until we do? Many don't, by the way; a lot slip off the mortal coil having learned bugger all."

"Come back again with harder lessons next time?"

"Probably."

"Shit. I've been a terrible traper, but it be too late now."

I'd had the wine glass pressed to my lips and spluttered all over the table.

"Sorry," she said, the lights in her eyes dancing. "I need to work on myself big time."

A glint in her eye for the gentlemen, Silas Finn had observed of Tamara, and then Ivy.

"Lots of mysteries, aren't there?" I said. "For instance, you and your mum don't look anything like the rest of the Hamlyn family. And I've since seen pictures of Tamara's sisters, and a huge photograph of all those at the big house back in 1870. There's only Tamara with those stunning looks. The rest look, um–"

"Like cabbage patch dolls?"

Again I spluttered. "Damn! Now I'll never get rid of that mental image. But yeah, bit blank-looking. I know what you mean."

"So what are you saying, Enys Quiller?"

She was laughing at me again, just as she had fifty years before.

"I don't know, just–"

"Maybe we're piskies? Infiltrators here to stir things up? Guess we'll never know the true nature of our being."

"Maybe you are. You've certainly got the mischievous gene."

"'Ere's what I want to know, though. And I'll tell you something now."

I laughed. "What?"

"Who the bloody hell was Silas Finn, then?"

We'd never talked about him, and her words had the effect of heavy stones dropping into a pond.

"Seriously, riddle me this, because I never saw him again after that Christmas in our barn. I came round to yours next day and you told me he'd visited. I heard your story and it was borne out with what we dug up. No doubt you seen him, right? And your parents too, or what happened later wouldn't have happened. Never thought anything more."

I had no idea what she was going to say, the only thing occurring to me all of a sudden, being we'd never discussed Silas Finn. We'd discussed what he'd said, but…

Oh my God, I do know what's coming…

"But when I was telling my mother about the old man who'd visited your place, I mentioned I'd seen him in the barn. She said she hadn't, and I must've been at the cider. Wasn't me who'd been at the cider, I'll tell you that now. Anyhow, again I didn't think too much of it, thought she'd not noticed, was all. But I'd been asking around for a while after what we found, grilling the oldies about Nancy Peller and Mad Mary, when I happened to innocently mention the old man again, that it'd been him who'd visited ee and I'd seen him later in the barn. Some of those fangle-toothed oldies must have been at least two hundred years old." She laughed again. "But, and this is why I never wanted to say anything, no one else saw him! I was the only one who saw him in the barn that Christmas and there must have been a hundred and fifty odd folks there that night."

"Ah!"

"I felt I must be going mad. I'd definitely seen him. Brought the subject up with my mother again and she said I was making up lies. I asked my dad, even one of the other fiddlers the following year, but no one else saw him, Enys. Turned out, and it was a slow dawning, I'll give ee that, but he'd not been seen by anyone else. Only me. But you saw him, so how could that be? Was he real or not? He must have been if you saw him. God, Enys, no one at our end believed me, said he wasn't there. And at your end you all seen him. Sent me into a spiral. My brain kept hitting a brick wall. If I asked you, you'd say of course he was real, we all seen him! So where did that leave me?

"I think all of the ghost stuff was at arm's length from me somehow, that it was happening in another house and wasn't real. I was busy helping to dig up a family injustice, to find the truth, but none of it ever truly hit home. Anyway, time went on and stories about the house came out from all sorts of people, and then you and I started talking and you told me about all those coincidences with the droll teller's story. I think that's why I wanted to stay in touch with you, because you were the only one I could talk to and I had this feeling one day we'd make sense of it. Anyway, I'll come to the point. Now you've confided in me I'll tell ee this, and I've kept it to myself all this time probably for the same reason you did, but I've run into all of the scrapers over the years since that Christmas, and none of them, not one, has ever heard of anyone called Silas Finn, or Connor or Gil. And they knows them all."

"You're joking!"

"No, I'm not joking, Enys Quiller."

"Well then," I said, downing another glass of wine in one go. "Silas Finn remains a mystery, Beatrice Hamlyn."

"Either that or we're both mad."

I told her then, about the lack of footprints.

"And you never told me this afore?"

"I couldn't. How could I? As far as I knew, you'd seen him and so had over a hundred other people. It was too–"

"All these years I've been scared half to death about it. But I saw him and the following morning I told you I had."

"Yes, you did. But as you say yourself, who believes us with something like that? They look at you as if you lost your mind. My parents refused to discuss it."

"So, he vanished into thin air? Not a trace?"

"Yes, yes he did."

Try as I might, I can't decide if the droll teller was for the good or the bad. At least a theory can be put forward for almost everything else, but who can explain the droll teller?

No one else saw him. Four of us did, though.

***

REFERENCES

1. A Taste for Poison' by Neil Bradbury
2. Cornish Folk Tales of Place: Traditional Stories from North East Cornwall by Anna Chorlton

More Books by Sarah England

Father of Lies

A Darkly Disturbing Occult Horror Trilogy: Book 1

Ruby is the most violently disturbed patient ever admitted to Drummersgate Asylum, high on the bleak moors of northern England. With no improvement after two years, Dr Jack McGowan finally decides to take a risk and hypnotises her. With terrifying consequences.
A horrific dark force is now unleashed on the entire medical team, as each in turn attempts to unlock Ruby's shocking and sinister past. Who is this girl? And how did she manage to survive such unimaginable evil? Set in a desolate ex-mining village, where secrets are tightly kept and intruders hounded out, their questions soon lead to a haunted mill, the heart of darkness… and the Father of Lies.

***

Tanners Dell - Book 2

Now only one of the original team remains – Ward Sister Becky. However, despite her fiancé, Callum, being unconscious and many of her colleagues either dead or critically ill, she is determined to rescue Ruby's twelve-year-old daughter from a similar fate to her mother.

But no one asking questions in the desolate ex-mining village Ruby hails from ever comes to a good end. And as the diabolical history of the area is gradually revealed, it seems the evil invoked is both real and contagious.

Don't turn the lights out yet!

***

Magda - Book 3

The dark and twisted community of Woodsend harbours a terrible secret – one tracing back to the age of the Elizabethan witch hunts, when many innocent women were persecuted and hanged.

But there is a far deeper vein of horror running through this village, an evil that, once invoked, has no intention of relinquishing its grip on the modern world. Rather, it watches and waits with focused intelligence, leaving Ward Sister Becky and CID Officer Toby constantly checking over their shoulders and jumping at shadows.

Just who invited in this malevolent presence? And is the demonic woman who possessed Magda back in the sixteenth century the same one now gazing at Becky whenever she looks in the mirror?

Are you ready to meet Magda in this final instalment of the trilogy? Are you sure?

***

The Owlmen

If They See You, They Will Come for You

Ellie Blake is recovering from a nervous breakdown. Deciding to move back to her northern roots, she and her psychiatrist husband buy Tanners Dell at auction – an old water mill in the moorland village of Bridesmoor.

However, there is disquiet in the village. Tanners Dell has a terrible secret, one so well guarded no one speaks its name. But in her search for meaning and very much alone, Ellie is drawn to traditional witchcraft and determined to pursue it. All her life she has been cowed. All her life she has apologised for her very existence. And witchcraft has opened a door she could never have imagined. Imbued with power and overawed with its magic, for the first time she feels she has come home, truly knows who she is.

Tanners Dell, though, with its centuries-old demonic history… well, it's a dangerous place for a novice…

***

The Soprano

A Haunting Supernatural Thriller

It is 1951 and a remote mining village on the North Staffordshire Moors is hit by one of the worst snowstorms in living memory. Cut off for over three weeks, the old and the sick will die, the strongest bunker down, and those with evil intent will bring to its conclusion a family vendetta spanning three generations.

Inspired by a true event, *The Soprano* tells the story of Grace Holland – a strikingly beautiful, much admired local celebrity who brings glamour and inspiration to the grimy moorland community. But why is Grace still here? Why doesn't she leave this staunchly Methodist, rain-sodden place and the isolated farmhouse she shares with her mother?

Riddled with witchcraft and tales of superstition, the story is mostly narrated by the Whistler family, who own the local funeral parlour, in particular six-year-old Louise – now an elderly lady – who recalls one of the most shocking crimes imaginable.

***

Hidden Company

A dark psychological thriller set in a Victorian asylum in the heart of Wales.

1893, and nineteen-year-old Flora George is admitted to a remote asylum with no idea why she is there, what happened to her child, or how her wealthy family could have abandoned her to such a fate. However, within a short space of time, it becomes apparent she must save herself from something far worse than that of a harsh regime.

2018, and forty-one-year-old Isobel Lee moves into the gatehouse of what was once the old asylum. A reluctant medium, it is with dismay she realises there is a terrible secret here – one desperate to be heard. Angry and upset, Isobel baulks at what she must now face. But with the help of local dark arts practitioner Branwen, face it she must.

This is a dark story of human cruelty, folklore and superstition. But the human spirit can and will prevail… unless of course, the wrath of the fae is incited…

***

Monkspike

You are not forgiven

1149 was a violent year in the Forest of Dean.

Today, nearly 900 years later, the forest village of Monkspike sits brooding. There is a sickness here passed down through ancient lines, one noted and deeply felt by Sylvia Massey, the new psychologist. What is wrong with Nurse Belinda Sully's son? Why did her husband take his own life? Why are the old people in Temple Lake Nursing Home so terrified? And what are the lawless inhabitants of nearby Wolfs Cross hiding?

It is a dark village indeed, but one which has kept its secrets well. That is, until local girl Kezia Elwyn returns home as a practising Satanist, and resurrects a hellish wrath no longer containable. Burdo, the white monk, will infest your dreams… This is pure occult horror and definitely not for the faint of heart…

***

Baba Lenka

Pure Occult Horror

1970, and *Baba Lenka* begins in an icy Bavarian village with a highly unorthodox funeral. The deceased is Baba Lenka, great-grandmother to Eva Hart. But a terrible thing happens at the funeral, and from that moment on everything changes for seven-year-old Eva. The family flies back to Yorkshire but it seems the cold Alpine winds have followed them home... and the ghost of Baba Lenka has followed Eva. This is a story of demonic sorcery and occult practices during the World Wars, the horrors of which are drip-fed into young Eva's mind to devastating effect. Once again, this is absolutely not for the faint of heart. Nightmares pretty much guaranteed...

***

Masquerade

A Beth Harper Supernatural Thriller Book 1

The first in a series of Beth Harper books, *Masquerade* is a supernatural thriller set in a remote North Yorkshire village. Following a whirlwind relocation for a live-in job at the local inn, Beth quickly realises the whole village is thoroughly haunted, the people here fearful and cowed. As a spiritual medium, her attention is drawn to Scarsdale Hall nearby, the enormous stately home dominating what is undoubtedly a wild and beautiful landscape. Built of black stone with majestic turrets, it seems to drain the energy from the land. There is, she feels, something malevolent about it, as if time has stopped…

***

Caduceus

Book Two in the Beth Harper Supernatural Thriller Series.

Beth Harper is a highly gifted spiritual medium and clairvoyant. Having fled Scarsdale Hall, she's drawn to the remote coastal town of Crewby in North West England, and it soon becomes apparent she has a job to do. The congeniality here is but a thin veneer masking decades of deeply embedded secrets, madness and fear. Although she has help from her spirit guides and many clues are shown in visions, it isn't until the senseless and ritualistic murders happen on Mailing Street, however, that the truth is finally unearthed. And Joe Sully, the investigating officer, is about to have the spiritual awakening of his life.

What's buried beneath these houses, though, is far more horrific and widespread than anything either of them could have imagined. Who is the man in black? What is the black goo crawling all over the rooftops? What exactly is The Gatehouse? And as for the local hospital, one night is more than enough for Beth... let alone three...

***

The Witching Hour

A Collection of thrillers, chillers and mysteries

The title story, *The Witching Hour*, inspired the prologue for *Father of Lies*. Other stories include *Someone Out There*, a three-part crime thriller set on the Yorkshire moorlands; *The Witchfinders*, a spooky 17th century witch hunt; and *Cold Melon Tart*, where the waitress discovers there are some things she simply cannot do. In *A Second Opinion*, a consultant surgeon is haunted by his late mistress; and *Sixty Seconds* sees a nursing home manager driven to murder. Whatever you choose, hopefully you'll enjoy the ride.

***

Groom Lake

A Dark Novella

Lauren Stafford, a traumatised divorcee, decides to rent a cottage on the edge of a beautiful ancestral estate in the Welsh Marches. But from the very first day of arrival, she instinctively knows there's something terribly wrong here – something malevolent and ancient – a feeling the whole place is trapped in a time warp. She really ought to leave. But the pull of the lake is too strong, its dark magic so powerful that it crosses over into dreams... turning them into nightmares. What lies beneath its still black surface? And why can't Lauren drag herself away? Why her? And why now?

***